I'd been wrong about him. He wasn't a player. He was sweet, caring, and genuine. So different from Matt that the two barely belonged in the same category of humankind. But then again, Patrick could have been a full-fledged saint and it wouldn't have mattered. I'd already told him I didn't date. Also, he'd made it crystal clear that his crush on me was history.

Which just brought me right back to my original question: Why was he being so nice to me? I needed to find out what was up, and I couldn't wait until Valentine's Day to do it, either.

ANNA HUMPHREY

Rhymes with Cupid

HarperTeen is an imprint of HarperCollins Publishers.

Rhymes with Cupid
 For information address HarperCollins Children's Books, a division of HarperCollins Publishers, 10 East 53rd Street, New York, NY 10022.
www.harperteen.com

Library of Congress catalog card number: 2010926432
ISBN 978-0-06-193501-5

11 12 13 14 15 CG/BV 10 9 8 7 6 5 4 3 2

First Edition

For Brent, my number-one valentine

Chapter 1

According to *The Itty Bitty Pocket Guide* (*Secrets of the Heart* edition), Cupid is the god of erotic love. He's the son of Aphrodite, the goddess of love and beauty, and Ares, the god of war. He's beautiful and mischievous and winged like an angel.

But at the SouthSide Mall in Middleford, Maine, Cupid was a far, far cry from the golden-haired god that the pocket guide (aisle four, right across from the ceramic clowns) described. He stood on the counter of Goodman's Gifts & Stationery near the cash register—an overweight battery-powered baby doll with shiny red hearts on his diaper. When you pushed his belly button, he winked a creepy mechanical eye at you and started to sing along to music that came out of a speaker in his butt—the chorus of the classic 1960s Motown hit, "Do You Love Me (Now That I Can Dance)." And the doll *could* dance, in a way. You had to give him that.

Cupid shook his diapered hips indecently, his plastic joints making a faint clicking noise as he swayed from side to side waving a plush bow and arrow in one hand while the music built in intensity. Finally, he closed the routine with another skeevy wink.

If Ares and Aphrodite could see what had become of their golden-haired son, they'd probably feel like throwing down a thunderbolt or two—unlike the masses at the mall who thought creepy mechanical dolls were adorable. Several dozen people had already bought enough greeting cards to earn their very own stupid singing Cupid through the customer loyalty program at the gift shop where I worked after school. We'd already placed our third order from the supplier.

"Oh. My. God." A woman approached the counter twirling a lock of her hair, which was severely teased and held back by a headband that was half zebra-, half leopard-print—what would you even call that animal? I wondered idly. A zepard? "Well, isn't that the cutest thing you've ever seen? Don't you just want to pinch him?"

I gave her my best neutral smile. Pinching Cupid wasn't exactly on my list of things to do. Now *pitching* him, I could handle. Right across the hall into the Gap, maybe. Or into one of the boat-sized garbage bins the janitorial staff pushed around at closing time.

She picked up the doll and hugged him to her chest before flipping him over to get a look at his unmentionables. "Does he take AAs?" she asked.

"Four Ds," I answered. Besides being annoying, the doll cost about twenty dollars in batteries to run. Money that could be *so* much better spent putting gas in her car, or groceries on her table, or even buying herself some stylish new animal-print headbands—giraffodile, maybe, or snakeetah?

"Oh, well now. Look here." She held the doll's butt up to my face. "You've got the switch flipped to the quiet setting. We can hardly hear his cute little song." Using a long, pink fingernail, she remedied the situation before setting Cupid back on the counter and pressing his tummy. He winked and started to sing again—five times louder. "You have a nice day now, you hear," the woman said.

"You too." I smiled as sincerely as I could manage. "Thanks for shopping at Goodman's." As soon as she'd turned her back and walked away into the brightly lit, overloud mall plaza, I let the smile drop from my face. Unfortunately, Cupid kept right on singing. "That's it," I shouted to my coworker Dina a few seconds later when she came out of the back room carrying a cardboard box. "We definitely need to kill this thing." I reached into the drawer for the scissors.

"Are you serious, Elyse?" she shouted back, her eyes growing wide. "You're going to stab Cupid?"

The doll winked again and finally fell silent. I laughed. "Actually, these are for the box." I held them up. "But, now that you mention it . . ."

"Elyse," Dina said softly, blinking her big brown eyes at me. "We probably shouldn't joke about damaging merchandise. Mr. Goodman would be really upset."

I should have known better than to kid about a thing like that with Dina. She was quite possibly the sweetest girl I'd ever met. So sweet that, sometimes, she was a bit nauseating—at least to someone as cynical as I'd been feeling lately. In the three months we'd been working together I'd lost count of how many times I'd caught her going all teary eyed over a clichéd love poem while shelving wedding cards.

"I'm kidding, Dina. Of course." I gave her an earnest look. "I would never do a thing like that to Cupid here." I patted his head to show I was sincere. "Or to anything else in the store." I motioned for her to pass me the box.

"Oh, obviously." She slid it down the counter. "I knew you were kidding. You're such a bighearted person, Elyse. Actually, that's partly why I've been meaning to ask you a favor." She leaned down and took a folder out of her backpack, which was stashed behind the cash. I caught a glimpse of a sad-looking baby panda on its cover. I could pretty much guess what was coming.

"I don't know if you knew this . . . but the giant panda is one of the world's most endangered species," Dina began, her voice cracking a little out of sympathy for all the threatened forest-dwelling bears of China. "Scientists think there are less than fifteen hundred of them left in the wild." She must have noticed that I was avoiding eye contact because she quickly added, "Just so you know, I'm not going to ask you for money."

I breathed a small sigh of relief. It wasn't that I had

anything against pandas (although, now that I thought of it, if you wanted to make a *really fancy* headband, you could combine a panda with a bald eagle . . . just kidding). The thing was, since my mom had lost her job six months earlier, part of my salary had been going to help with household expenses. Even now that she'd found a new job (which she was starting that afternoon), there wouldn't be a ton to spare. Plus, I'd sponsored Dina in a knit-a-thon to help stop the slaughter of sheep just a month before. Since then, I'd had to avoid getting the curried lamb special at India House in the food court, and it was my favorite.

"I'm organizing a panda party," she explained, "for Valentine's Day. We'll all wear black and white, and each guest will make a donation to Panda Rescue. I'm hoping we can raise five hundred dollars to cosponsor a panda for the year. This one is Oreo." She pulled a picture out of her folder. I tried to avert my gaze—no need to get swept away by the panda's inevitable cuteness. "I know you're good at baking, Elyse. My family practically inhaled those cookies you gave us at Christmas. So, I was wondering, would you make black-and-white snacks for the party?"

I hesitated. After all, making food for a panda party would put a crimp in my big plans for February 14. I was going to buy five boxes of heart-shaped chocolates using my employee discount and eat them all in one sitting to drown my sorrows.

"I don't know," I said. "I'll probably be busy that night."

"With a guy?" Dina asked eagerly.

"No. Just, you know, with my mom. I don't want her to be all alone on Valentine's Day." That much was true. Well, partly true, anyway.

The whole truth was this: I'd been betrayed last Valentine's Day by the former two-most-important people in my life. So it was no surprise I'd been looking forward to the love fest with the kind of dread I usually reserved for dental fillings and driving lessons. All I wanted to do was hide in my house and wait for all the happy togetherness of the holiday to be over with—not to mention for all the singing Cupids to be silenced.

And working at Goodman's wasn't helping matters. Every time I picked up a tacky pink teddy bear or shelved a heart-shaped card, my mind drifted back to where I'd been this time last year—so happy, and so much in love—then compared it to where I was this year—alone, and still more than a little brokenhearted.

See, exactly one year ago, I had a boyfriend. His name—ironically enough—was Matt Love. We'd met in chemistry class in September of tenth grade while doing a lab. We had to calculate the moles of water we'd just removed and the moles of magnesium sulfate left in our solution. He had no idea what he was doing.

"There are moles in that beaker?" he'd said. "So what did they do? Dig them out of their mole holes and liquefy them? Nasty." At first I thought he was kidding, so I laughed, but then I saw that he was actually serious.

"Moles are a unit of measurement in chemistry," I

explained, fixing him with a steady stare.

"Oh yeah?"

"Yeah."

"Huh. Who knew? You're smart, aren't you? Pretty, too."

I'd always considered myself average. I was thin in a tomboyish way, with straight brown hair and brown eyes with tiny blue flecks in them. I wore glasses. I wasn't the kind of girl guys flirted with, unless they wanted someone to review their English essay or help them with calculus. I'd had no idea how to respond to Matt's comment, but it didn't seem to matter. He'd already decided that he liked me, and he was determined to keep pursuing me with puppy-dog-like enthusiasm until I started liking him back.

"You're insane, you know that, right?" my then-best-friend Tabby told me the third time I turned down Matt Love's invitation to see a movie over the weekend. "He's gorgeous. And popular. Funny, too. Plus, he has his own car. I'm just saying. . . ."

If I could travel back in time, I'd tell Tabby that if she thought he was so great, she should have gone out with him. It would have saved us all a lot of trouble, and me a lot of heartache. But, instead, the short version of what happened is that, eventually, Matt Love wore me down.

I started noticing the cuteness of his slapstick brand of humor, and the hotness of his smile, instead of the lowness of his IQ. I *did* go out with him. And he was gorgeous, and popular just like Tabby said. We were a weird match—the cautious, brainy girl and the total goofball popular guy—but we worked. He introduced me to Jackie Chan movies and taught me how to spit watermelon seeds really far. He gave me my first real kiss, and then my second, and my third. He even let me drive his car once (which, trust me, was a very bad idea). And, meanwhile, I helped him bring his chemistry grade up from a D to a solid B-minus.

But it all ended on Valentine's Day when I walked into my room, expecting to find Tabby there. Matt and I had a date (the new Jackie Chan movie followed by dinner at Flapjack's—his favorite pancake restaurant), and Tabby, who was good at that kind of thing, was going to go to my place right after school and pick out an outfit for me while I finished my tutoring session. And, in some ways, she didn't let me down.

When I got home, Tabby was in my room, like she said she'd be. And she'd picked out an outfit and laid it on the bed, like she'd promised she would. It's just that she happened to be lying on top of the outfit, and Matt Love—who had obviously arrived early to pick me up—happened to be lying on top of her. And as for how the rest of my Valentine's Day went, you can pretty much guess.

Dina carefully moved aside Styrofoam packing in the box I'd just opened and lifted out a picture frame. "Awwww. Look." She showed me. It was pink and had pictures of daisies and sunflowers running up the sides. Across the top it read in swirly script: *Like a well-tended garden . . .* Then it continued on the bottom: *. . . our love grows stronger every day.* I tried not to gag.

Suddenly the look on Dina's face went from gushy to sad. I braced myself. "You know what this would have been perfect for?" she asked, then answered her own question. "This photo of me and Damien I have."

I nodded in what I hoped seemed like a comforting way but, secretly, I was glancing at the clock. There were two more hours left before the store closed. I wasn't sure if I'd be able to stand that much Damien talk.

"We asked this homeless man at the botanical gardens to take it for us last summer," Dina explained. "Damien thought he was going to run off with our camera, but I said, 'Just because he doesn't have a place to live, doesn't mean he's not a good person.' And I'm so glad we asked. That photo's one of my favorites. I'll bring it tomorrow to show you."

"Great," I said. "That would be great." I'd already seen pictures of Damien standing on the sidewalk. Pictures of Damien eating hamburgers. Pictures of Damien taking pictures of Dina, who was taking pictures of him. It was pretty amazing how many pictures of Damien Dina had, especially when you considered she'd only dated him for three weeks last summer before he'd dumped her and gone off to college. "I'd love to see that photo. But, Dina . . ." I chose my next words carefully. "Do you think it's maybe time you started seeing other people? Or, at least, thinking about seeing other people?" She clutched the picture frame against her chest. "I mean, Damien's dating someone else."

The mere mention of the other girl made Dina's eyes glaze over with tears, and I felt horrible for bringing it up. If anyone knew what it was like to have your heart broken by a guy, it was me.

"He's not *really* dating her," Dina corrected. "They're just seeing each other. Casually."

"Right," I said. "That's what I meant. But you know, Dina," I went on, "there's no reason you can't see someone else casually, too." I lifted a stack of frames out of the box, counted them, and checked them off against the packing slip. "At least consider it. You never know who you might meet."

I managed to say the words with authority, but even as I doled out the advice, I knew I was being a hypocrite. Just that morning, over breakfast, my mom had suggested I introduce myself to the guy next door. My reaction was less than positive.

"He's out there shoveling the driveway for his grandfather right now," she'd said. "I even saw him put down salt on the icy patches. He seems like a very responsible boy. I'm not saying date him," my mom added quickly, when I shot her a weary look. She knew all too well how devastated I'd been after the whole Matt Love/Tabby disaster. I'd hardly left the house for weeks, and I'd been entirely too excited about changing high schools and leaving all my classmates behind last September in preparation for our move to a smaller, cheaper house on the other side of town. Anything to get away from the sight of my ex and former best friend holding hands in the hallways, making googly eyes in geography, and kissing in the cafeteria while I sat with some girls from advanced math who I barely knew, pretending to be absorbed in algorithms.

"But at least say hello to him on your way out. You really never know," my mom added with an encouraging look. Except I *did* know. I didn't care how much salt the boy next door put on the driveway. I wasn't interested in meeting him—or any other guy. I had my mom to talk to at home, and Dina to talk to at work. At my new school, I sat with Dina and some of her friends at lunch, and besides that I kept to myself and studied hard. I liked it that way. Plus, if I wanted to go to college, I'd need a full scholarship. I had important goals to focus on and I wasn't about to let another broken heart slow me down now. There'd be plenty of time for dating when I was older, anyway. Why waste time on high school guys?

But Dina was a different story. She was sulking over Damien like there would never be another guy who could compare. It was sad, to tell the truth. What she needed was a distraction, and fast.

"You're a great person, Dina. You deserve a guy who's going to love you back. Someone who's going to really be there for you."

Her eyes softened. "Seriously, Elyse? You think that? That's one of the nicest things anyone has ever said to me.

But . . ." She paused, resting her elbows against the counter. "Damien is the one for me. Actually, I was thinking about calling him tonight. . . ."

I envisioned our shift the next day. How she'd come in with bags under her eyes after being up all night crying over something Damien had or *hadn't* said to her. How, while restocking the shelves, she'd want me to help her analyze each and every sentence, looking for hidden meanings and hoping beyond hope that he still cared about her when he so clearly, clearly didn't.

"No," I said too forcefully. She looked up. "You can't call Damien. Dina, you have to let him go."

And, just like that, the answer to all my problems walked into the store, pausing at the circular rack that held novelty key chains. He was tall and lean, dressed in a soft-looking plaid shirt. He wore a pair of supergiant DJ-style earphones around his neck. His skin was freckled and his dark hair was a mess of curls. He leaned in close and, if I wasn't mistaken, looked at his reflection in the edge of the metallic shelf divider to check for food between his teeth.

"Oh my God," I said. "It's like a sign." Dina glanced around, confused. "That guy who just walked into the store," I whispered. "He was checking you out."

Chapter 2

"Really? He was checking me out?" Dina looked over nervously at the guy, who was using his fingernail to dislodge a piece of lettuce, or something, from between his front teeth.

He *wasn't* checking her out. But then, she didn't need to know that. Dina was a pretty girl. Not to mention ridiculously nice. Any guy would consider himself lucky to meet her. I was sure of it.

"He totally was. You should go over and talk to him."

For half a second, Dina looked like she was thinking about it, but then she hesitated. "I can't. What about Damien?"

"Who cares about Damien?" I said sharply, then reminded myself to be nice. "Anyway, you'd just be doing your job. Helping a customer."

"You're right," she said, giving her head a tiny shake. "He's just a customer."

"Exactly. Just a *cute* customer. Go see what he needs. And why don't you ask for his phone number while you're over there?"

"What?!" she exclaimed.

"Just ask him. See what happens. Look, I'll make you a deal. If you ask him, I'll bake pinwheel cookies for your panda party."

She seemed to be weighing her options.

"*And* a chocolate and vanilla cheesecake. *And* I'll donate twenty-five dollars at the door. That's, like, one twentieth of a bear, all in exchange for a measly phone number. Come on," I teased. "Do it for Oreo. Plus," I added in a moment of desperation, "Damien will be jealous when he hears you got another guy's number."

Before I even finished my plea, my very favorite customer, an older Italian woman named Mrs. Conchetti, walked into the store. She shopped at Goodman's at least once a week, buying kitschy mini figurines and corny wall plaques that said things like "A mother's love knows no bounds" and "Home is where the heart is." Her entire house must have looked like a shrine to tackiness. But she was really sweet, and always laughing. Plus, we shared a love of homemade desserts. Sometimes she brought me fresh panettone bread, just because she knew how much I liked it.

"Oh, he's so cute I could eat him up," she squealed as she stepped up to the counter and set down an armload of Valentine's Day cards. Dina glanced at the tooth-checking guy a second time, not noticing that Mrs. Conchetti was actually grinning at the stupid Cupid.

"I'm doing it," Dina said bravely. "He *is* cute. Plus, if

Damien can see somebody else casually, I can flirt with a guy. Why not?" She reached out to press Cupid's tummy. "Hey," she added, when I rolled my eyes and picked him up to readjust the volume setting, "a little help from Cupid never hurt anyone, right?"

Dina strode confidently across the shop floor headed directly for the guy, who had wandered over to one of the Valentine's Day card displays.

As soon as she'd gone, Mrs. Conchetti slid her customer loyalty card across to me. "How many does that make now, Elyse, dear?" she asked as I stamped her purchases.

"We give a stamp for every five. So you'll need to buy another ten cards to earn the Cupid." She looked down at her wallet, clearly disappointed. "They don't have to be valentines though," I explained. "Birthday cards count, too. Or anniversary cards. Even bereavement cards." Her face brightened.

"That's wonderful news," she said. "I'll be back next week after I get my check. It never hurts to plan ahead for special occasions." She counted on her fingers. "If I buy five cards a week I'll have this doll for my grandson in time for his birth. It's just perfect. My daughter's due on Valentine's Day, you know. She's having a boy." I *did* know. Mrs. Conchetti had bought the powder-blue birth announcements almost two months ago, and she'd already picked out three Precious Moments figurines for the baby's room. To say she was kind of excited about the arrival of her first grandchild would be an understatement—like saying I was a touch irritated by Cupid.

"That'll be thirty-two dollars and fifty-seven cents." I tried to see around Mrs. Conchetti as she counted out the money, hoping for a glimpse of Dina and the guy, but they'd disappeared down another aisle.

"Have a wonderful day, Mrs. Conchetti," I said, handing over her shopping bag full of cards. "I'll see you soon."

"You will!" She reached out to tweak Cupid's plush cheek, then pressed his tummy to start him up one more time.

I opened the drawer to put the scissors away before I could be tempted to hurt the charming little cherub after all, then leaned down to watch Dina and the guy on the security camera behind the desk. They were in the office supply aisle now, where Dina was leaning forward, looking kind and welcoming—genuinely interested in whatever tooth-checking guy was saying. She tucked her hair behind one ear in a flirty way and leaned in to listen again. I had to hand it to her. Even if she was only doing it for the pandas, Dina was braver than I would have given her credit for—much braver than I was, at least, when it came to looking for love. Although, now that I thought about it, maybe that wasn't saying a whole lot.

"I can't believe how nice he was," Dina said for about the third time that afternoon as we slid down the metal grate to lock up the store. "And he's *so* cute. How did I never notice him before?"

It seemed the tooth-checking guy (whose name turned out to be Patrick) had been working at the Keyhole—a key-cutting kiosk near the frozen yogurt stand—for the past six months. He went to Collingwood Tech—the high school for students who planned to go into trades like carpentry or auto mechanics—which explained why we didn't know him from school. "He said we should come by sometime, whenever we're on break. I totally think I'm going to." Dina checked her reflection in her compact while I pulled the store keys out of my bag.

Luckily for me, Dina hadn't managed to work up the nerve to ask the guy for his phone number, saving me from having to make the $25 donation I couldn't really afford anyway. "I think I might even invite him to the panda party. But I'm not going to tell Damien. I mean, at least not yet. Do you think that's okay?"

"Of course it's okay. You just met the guy. All you're doing is getting to know him. Not that it's any of Damien's business anyway. He's not your boyfriend anymore. You're a free woman." She nodded, but didn't look completely convinced.

We headed for the east doors, waving to the girls who were closing up the Gap. "What was he looking at, anyway?" I asked. "I mean, besides you?" She smacked me lightly, but it was obvious she was enjoying being teased.

"He needed a new pen."

"But then he never bought one," I pointed out.

"I think his break was probably ending. Oh no," she said and clapped a hand over her mouth. "I was talking to him so much that he never got to buy his pen. What if he really needed it?"

"I'm sure he'll be okay," I said. "The world is full of pens. And, anyway, it gives him an excuse to come back again tomorrow."

She smiled. "Are you sure you don't want a ride home?" Dina asked as we reached the doors. "It's, like, minus twenty out there. And that's before the windchill."

"I'm sure," I reassured her. "You live in the opposite direction. Anyway, the bus goes right by our new house."

She nodded. "As long as you're sure. See you tomorrow, okay? And thanks for encouraging me to talk to that guy. You're a really good friend, Elyse."

"So are you," I said as I waved good-bye, and I meant it. Since I'd changed schools in September, I hadn't met very many people. In a way, I guess I hadn't wanted to. Thanks to last year's aforementioned disastrous February 14, I'd sort of been off close friendships, and boys, and trusting people in general.

"Dammit." I sighed, stepping off the curb to cross the mall parking lot. The cold air stung my eyes as I watched the number four bus roar past, spraying gray sludgy snow in all directions. I pulled my coat sleeve up to check my watch. The number four ran once every half hour. It was seven fifteen. That meant I wouldn't get home until after eight, and it was already dark. The security guard locked the mall doors from the outside at seven sharp every weeknight, too, so there was no way to get back inside where it was warm. I should have taken Dina up on her way-too-kind offer of a ride home, after all.

Resigning myself to a long, cold wait, I dug my mittened hands into my coat pockets and crossed the street to the bus shelter where I sank down onto the tiny metal bench. There was a poster enclosed in the glass on one side advertising Mexican vacations, and I stared at it longingly as I waited, hating the happy couple enjoying fruity beverages in their bathing suits. Seriously, whose idea of a cruel joke had it been to put that in a bus shelter in the middle of winter?

"You got a cigarette?" I jumped at the sound of the voice and looked up to see a man in a brown jacket with two rips in the side. Some of the stuffing was falling out, and one of his shoelaces was broken, leaving his boot hanging open. His feet must have been freezing, not to mention wet.

"Sorry," I said. "I don't smoke."

He kind of grunted. "You got any change?"

I shook my head. All I had was my bus fare.

"Come on," he pressed. "A few quarters at least. I'm hungry." By this time, he'd come into the bus shelter and was standing over me. He was so close that I could smell the alcohol on his breath.

I tried to seem calm. It wasn't that I'd never seen a homeless person before—I'd just never seen one this close up. The old downtown area, where my mom and I had lived until a week ago, was quaint and touristy. Panhandlers got shooed away by the shopkeepers and police pretty quickly.

My heart was pounding in fear, but I tried to remember what Dina had said about her homeless photographer. Just because this guy looked like he didn't have a place to live, didn't mean he was a bad person. I took a deep breath, determined to be brave.

"I'm really sorry," I said again.

"Sure you are," the man answered. I glanced up and down the deserted street, hoping to see the bus coming in the distance, or at least another person who might hear me if I had to yell for help.

"A bill, then. You got a few dollar bills?" I shook my head again. My heartbeat went up another notch as the man started kicking angrily at the ground, dislodging bits of ice with the toe of his boot and sending them in my direction.

"I'm sorry," I said again. "If I had extra money, I'd give it to you. I swear." A chunk of ice hit my shin and I yelped, more in panic than in pain. "Okay, fine. Here." I pulled my mitten off and slid my hand into my coat pocket, about to take out my bus fare and give it to him. I didn't know what I'd tell my mom when I had to call her for a ride on her very first day of work, but all I wanted was for the man to leave me alone. I'd worry about that later.

"Jack!" I heard somebody call as my hand closed

around the coins. A red car pulled up, slowing at the bus stop, and a guy leaned out the window. "What's the problem? Are you bothering her?" It wasn't until the homeless man turned that I got a clear view of the person in the car: Patrick—Dina's tooth-checking, pen-buying guy—his curls sticking out from under a blue-and-white wool hat.

"I was just asking for a little change," the man grumbled. "For something to eat. She's got money. I hear it in her pocket."

"Come on," Patrick said. "Leave her alone. Look." He took out his wallet. "I've got a five. I give this to you, you go get a burger, you leave her alone. Deal?"

The homeless guy walked up to the car window, took the bill, and mumbled his thanks before starting off down the street.

"You okay?" Patrick asked, leaning out his window again. The white pom-pom on his hat bobbed when he tilted his head.

"Of course," I said, trying to keep my voice even. After all, it's not like anybody ever died from having ice chips kicked at them. I hadn't been in any danger. "He wasn't really bothering me."

"Okay," he said, but I could tell he didn't believe me. "You want a ride somewhere? It's pretty cold to be waiting for the bus. And I'm going your way."

How did he know which way I was going? I wondered. But then, feeling like an idiot, I realized that I was waiting for the southbound bus. Obviously, I was going south. I shook my head. I knew way better than to get in a car with some strange guy, even if Dina thought he seemed nice, and even if the alternative was waiting in the dark, in an Arctic deep freeze by myself. "Thanks. I'm good though. The bus will be here in twenty minutes."

"Want me to wait with you?" he offered. "In case Jack comes back. He's harmless, but sometimes he has a bit of a temper when he's hungry. You might have noticed."

"No. Thanks," I said, wishing he'd just leave. It was embarrassing enough that he'd seen how clearly afraid I'd been. "Honestly, I'm fine."

"Okay." He hesitated. "Are you sure?" he asked.

"I already told you," I said, failing to hide my annoyance now. "I'm sure."

"Okay then . . . if you're really sure. I'll see you around. Maybe at work tomorrow, if you and Dina have a shift." I was surprised that he'd even recognized me from the store. After all, he'd spent the whole time talking to Dina and hadn't come up to the cash register.

"Yeah, maybe." I shrugged before digging my hands back into my pockets. He rolled up his window and pulled away slowly.

Okay, that was weird, I thought. But then again, at least I'd have a few things to tell Dina about her guy at work the next day . . . like that he was nice to the point of annoyingness, and that he had a soft spot for homeless people. Honestly, he and Dina were going to be perfect for each other. I watched as he drove down the street before doing a U-turn and circling back through the parking lot of the mall. He pulled into a space facing the road and turned off his headlights. At first I thought he must have forgotten something at the Keyhole. But Dina said he'd been working there for six months. Didn't he know the main doors to the mall would be locked? Then five minutes passed. Then ten. Why wasn't he getting out of the car?

And that was about when I figured it out: He *was* waiting to make sure I got on the bus safely. I couldn't help it; I gritted my teeth. Hadn't I *told* him I was fine? It's not like I needed some kind of knight in shining armor to swoop in and save me. I was a smart, independent seventeen-year-old girl—perfectly capable of taking care of myself.

I stood up and walked to the curb, trying to catch his eye. It was hard to see all the way across the street and through his darkened windshield, but I could make out the white of his pom-pom. A second later, he glanced up and I waved to get his attention. When he waved back I glared at him, making a shooing motion with my hand. "Go home, you idiot," I said, even though I knew he obviously couldn't hear me. "I'm fine. Leave." He shrugged like he didn't understand. "Go home!!" I said, shooing him again. He rolled down the window and leaned out.

"What?" he shouted.

"I said I'm really fine. You can go," I yelled back.

"Sorry. Didn't catch that," he answered, cupping a hand around his ear. I rolled my eyes.

"Go!" I shouted as loudly as I possibly could. "Go, go, go!"

"Snow? Oh! Snow!" he yelled back. I'd swear he was grinning. "Snow, snow, snow. Yeah. There's a lot of it. Happens every winter." He waved. "See you tomorrow," he called before rolling his window back up and continuing to sit in his car, going nowhere.

I stamped my feet on the sidewalk, partly to keep them warm, but mostly out of frustration. I couldn't have yelled it any louder or been any clearer with my hand gestures. He was purposely ignoring me, which was rude beyond belief. I was actually considering marching across the street and straight up to his car window to yell it again when I saw the headlights of the bus in the distance. It was running five minutes early, but I wasn't about to complain.

"It's a chilly one out there," the bus driver quipped as I climbed on.

"Definitely cold," I answered, stamping the snow off my boots and dumping my change into the slot before glancing over the driver's shoulder. In the parking lot, the lights of Patrick-the-pen-guy's car came on. I glared in his direction as he started to back out of the spot, his tires spinning against the snow. I hoped he'd get stuck.

"Cold is right." The driver laughed. "I'd even go as far as to say frosty." The bus lurched forward and I turned my eyes away from the red car's headlights, stumbling down the aisle to find a seat.

Chapter 3

"Where have you been?" My mother greeted me at the front door. She pressed both hands against my cheeks. "Are you okay? You're just frozen. Come inside. Did you have to wait long for the bus?"

"I'm fine, Mom," I said as I let her help me out of my coat. I took my fogged-up glasses off, wiping them clean on the front of my shirt. "How was your first day at work?"

"Oh, well." She shook the snow off my jacket and hung it up. "It was eye-opening. Elyse, you wouldn't believe the things people pay good money for. Have you ever heard of a mustard wrap?" I shook my head. "Me neither," she sighed. "A woman came in asking for one. I thought it was a kind of sandwich and I told her we didn't serve food. Well, I've never been so embarrassed in my life."

After ten years of dedicated service, my mom had been laid off from her job as a filing clerk for an auto insurance company the May before. She'd spent the last eight months looking for work. Needless to say, when she was offered the position of receptionist at a fancy downtown spa, she'd jumped at the opportunity—even though it paid less, and even though she'd never set foot in a place like that before in her life. Ever since I was five and my dad fell in love with his dental hygienist and moved to Calgary, my mom has had to work hard to support us. And even though my dad sent child support money, and my mom put in long hours to make sure she could give me everything else I needed, our life wasn't exactly full of luxury.

"Some of the clients are a bit demanding, of course, but that's nothing I'm not used to. One of them complained that her robe wasn't fluffy enough and asked to speak to the manager." My mom laughed. "But the other staff seems nice. That's enough about my day, though," she finished. "You look tired, sweetie. Come into the kitchen. I made tacos. I was expecting you sooner, so they're a little cold. I'll pop them in the microwave." I sank down at the table gratefully.

"How was the bus ride?" my mom asked as she slid a plate into the microwave. "Did it take long? I hate to think of you waiting in the dark and the cold."

"It was fine," I lied, not wanting to tell her that I still couldn't feel my toes, or that I'd had ice kicked at me by a scary homeless man. It would only worry her and make her feel guilty that she couldn't make it to the mall on time to pick me up anymore. "I just missed the first bus, so I had to wait a little longer."

"Well, you won't have to take the bus much longer. I booked you another road test. Two weeks from tomorrow," she said as she set a plate down in front of me.

"Mom!" I cried.

"It was one thing when we were living in old Middleford and everything was close by, but out here you need your license, Elyse. That way you can take the car for the day and I can ride the bus. It's a shorter trip for me anyway."

I sighed. It wasn't only that I'd feel guilty driving while my mom waited for public transit. It was also that I was officially parallel-parking-impaired, not to mention a total menace to public safety. The last time I was at the DMV, I got so nervous that I accidentally pressed the gas instead of the brake and drove right through a construction barrier.

"I think there's a limit, Mom. They only let you fail that test so many times before they officially ban you from the roads." I poked a piece of lettuce back into my taco.

"Oh, I have a good feeling. You'll pass this time." She smiled mischievously. "I've arranged for some extra help."

"Mom!" I cried again. I'd already taken the defensive driver's course twice (at $500 a shot), plus, I'd failed the road test a total of three times (another $300). We literally couldn't afford to waste any more money trying to teach me to drive, especially when it was so clearly a lost cause.

"I was talking with Mr. Connor next door this morning. His grandson passed his test on the first try. And he's eighteen, which means he has two years of driving experience." I grimaced, already anticipating where this was going. "Mr. Connor spoke to his grandson, and it turns out he'd be glad to help you prepare for your test over the next few weeks. No charge."

"Mom. I'm sure Mr. Connor's grandson has other things he'd rather be doing."

"Oh, I doubt that," my mom said, lifting her taco. The reheated shell had gone soggy in the microwave and most of the filling spilled out, landing on her plate. She scooped it back in, undeterred. "I think any young man would be grateful for an excuse to meet the pretty girl who just moved in next door." I shot her a doubtful look. "Plus, it would be good for you to make some new friends, Elyse. I'm concerned about you. You barely go out with people your own age anymore."

"I'm fine, Mom. Just busy. With work. And school. Speaking of which . . ." I stood up, putting my plate on the counter. "I have a calculus test I should probably study for."

"All right," she said. "Well, I'm just going to clean up here. Then I have those hooks to install in the bathroom, and I'll get started on sanding down that wardrobe in the basement so we can unpack the rest of our winter clothes." She rubbed at her eyes when she thought I wasn't looking, then smiled when she noticed I was still watching.

Forget being concerned about me. My mom was the one who really needed someone to worry about her. The stress of looking for a new job, selling the house, and arranging the move had taken a toll on her. She looked tired, and way too thin. I glanced down at the table. She'd barely taken two bites of her taco but she'd already started running the tap to fill the sink and was busy putting away the leftover chopped tomatoes.

"I'll come help you sand the wardrobe when I'm done

studying, okay?" I said.

"Sounds great." She smiled. "Oh, and Elyse?"

I turned.

"Before I forget to tell you, Mr. Connor's grandson is going to come by at six o'clock tomorrow for your lesson. I'll be at work, but he said you could use his car." My mom looked so optimistic that I didn't have the heart to argue with her anymore.

"How's his insurance policy?" I asked instead.

"He's with Slate Auto," my mom answered. "Full coverage." Somehow, I'd known that she would have thought to check. In a million tiny ways, my mother was always, always looking out for me.

I spent a lot of the next day at school daydreaming (or maybe I should say daynightmaring) about the different ways I might accidentally crash my neighbor's car into trees, oncoming traffic, or innocent pedestrians. Clearly, the poor guy had had no idea what he was getting into when he'd let his grandfather volunteer him for this job, but he was going to find out soon.

"Ah, girls. Right on time as always," Mr. Goodman said, looking up over his reading glasses as Dina and I walked into the store for our shift that day. He stepped out from behind the counter, taking off his name tag. Mr. Goodman's wife always had an early dinner waiting for him, so he never hung around for long after we arrived.

"The new shipment of Cupids came in," he told us. I tried not to jump for joy. "And the rest of the Valentine's

Day card order. Our sales are down this year, so I need you girls to really push the customer loyalty program. Make sure everyone who walks through the door knows how easy it is to get one of these cute little fellas." He patted Cupid's head. "Can I count on you?" We both nodded. I wasn't looking forward to pushing the dolls but, on the upside, at least if we sold them all, they'd be gone.

We got to work. Dina started on cash while I restocked merchandise. It was boring work, but kind of soothing in a way—matching cards and envelopes and sliding them into their perfectly organized slots. I started with congratulations and birthdays and was on the last batch of valentines when I heard a voice behind me.

"Hi. Can you help me? I'm looking for a new pen." I turned, and there was Patrick, Dina's guy.

He had his thumb hooked into one pocket of his dark-wash jeans and was tilting his head to the side, his curls falling over one eye in a way that, illogically, made my heart skip the tiniest beat. His green eyes twinkled kindly. But then he grinned, and there was something about that overly confident smile that reminded me of the night before in the parking lot.

"I'd be happy to tell you about our selection of pens," I answered in a pleasant voice, then gave him a tight smile, "but I have a feeling you wouldn't listen to a word I was saying anyway." The grin fell from his face leaving a shocked expression behind. "I'm talking about last night," I filled him in, helpfully, in case there was any confusion, "when I said I was okay, but you sat in the parking lot watching me anyway."

"What makes you think I was watching you?" he answered, his mouth dropping open.

"The fact that you were sitting in your car, in the empty parking lot, looking at me."

He paused. "Okay. I was sitting in my car, in the empty parking lot," he countered, "but it was because I wanted to write something down before I forgot it. If you were in front of me, and I looked up, it was purely coincidental."

"Right," I said, shelving a sparkly heart card, then shaking my hands to un-glitter them. "And I'd totally believe you were sitting in your car, in the cold, writing in the dark . . . except that I happen to know for a fact that you don't have a pen."

He smiled again—a small, quick expression that he wiped off his face the second he saw I'd turned around. I smiled back, enjoying the fact that I'd caught him in his obvious lie.

"You're right," he admitted. "I don't have a pen. That's why I always carry this." He slid something small and black out of his pocket and held it up. "A mini cassette recorder. So, I wasn't *writing,* technically, I guess."

I raised my eyebrows. "What are you? An undercover reporter or something?"

"No," he answered, but he didn't elaborate.

"An international spy?" I tried.

"You have a good imagination," he said. I must have still been looking at him strangely. "I'm a songwriter," he explained, then glanced down awkwardly. "Or, I want to be one someday. I'm kind of in this band—The Duotangs—with my friend Jax, but we're not that good, or anything. We just started. Anyway, I use this to record tunes or lyrics that pop into my head."

"Oh. Okay," I said, feeling like the world's biggest—not to mention most egotistical—jerk. "That's cool. I mean, sorry."

"Not that I wouldn't have waited for you to get on the bus safely if you'd wanted me to," he added, giving me a look I thought seemed almost flirty, but only until I came to my senses. He wasn't flirting with me, obviously, just like he hadn't been trying to act like some knight in shining armor yesterday. He was just a guy, who wrote songs. A *very embarrassed* guy who wrote songs, too, judging by how flushed his freckled cheeks had suddenly become.

"Really," I said, "I'm really sorry." An awkward silence hung between us. "About that pen you needed." I motioned toward the stationery aisle. He ended up going with the very first one I suggested, the EasyGrip in black—definitely one of our more expensive pens. "Dina at the cash can help you with that," I said, grateful that we were almost finished. I could hardly look him in the eye. "And be sure to ask her about the customer loyalty plan, okay?" I added, remembering Mr. Goodman's request.

"Sure," he said, then held up the pen. "Thanks. See you soon."

The second he turned his back I made a dash for the storage room, planning to rearrange some of the overstock until he was safely out of the store.

"I chickened out!" Dina said ten minutes later, when I went to take over at the cash. "Patrick came back to get a pen, and I was totally going to ask him to the panda party. I swear, Elyse, I was this close, and then this song came on the radio—'Against All Odds.' Damien and I slow danced to it once in my bedroom, and then I just couldn't get the words out."

"That's okay, Dina," I said reassuringly. "You know, maybe it's for the best. Maybe you just aren't ready yet." The truth was, I knew myself well enough to know I'd probably end up making the black-and-white snacks and going to Dina's panda party. The last thing I needed, after having acted like such a loser, was to be in a confined space with the cute pen guy, celebrating cuddly endangered bears on Valentine's Day. In fact, I was planning to cut frozen yogurt out of my diet completely and take the longer route to the bathrooms just so I'd never have to pass the Keyhole and risk seeing him again.

"Maybe you're right. Maybe I'm not ready," Dina mused. "Except he *is* really cute. You have to admit." Actually, I didn't have to admit it. I didn't have to admit it at all because it was of literally no consequence. He had his pen now. There was no reason for him to come back. "Oh," Dina said suddenly. "I think that woman in the parka needs help. Plus, I have to tell her about Cupid. See you in a sec."

She dashed off, leaving me at the cash register, where I started ringing up sale after sale. In fact, the store got so busy that I almost (but not quite) forgot to rehash the embarrassing incident in my head, or to dread my upcoming driving lesson until I looked up and saw Sue, one of the Friday night shift girls, walking into the store.

This time I managed to catch the first bus, getting to the stop with seconds to spare. I was home in time to make myself an omelet and unpack a few boxes of books before the doorbell rang.

"Coming," I called as I shrugged on my coat. I took a deep breath to gather the courage I'd need for the perilous lesson ahead and opened the door.

My new neighbor was standing in the driveway, brushing off the windshield of his red car, his back turned to me. "You must be Mr. Connor's grandson," I said, then tried to make a joke. "I hope you're ready for a wild ride."

He turned. I froze—and not because of the temperature, which was a bone-chilling -25 with windchill. "You're Mr. Connor's grandson?" I said. The pom-pom of his blue and white hat bobbed when he nodded his head.

"And you're Elyse," Patrick said simply, as if he wasn't surprised. He must have noticed the shocked look on my face because he went on. "We kind of met the night you moved in, remember? You saw me through the window."

I shook my head.

"I waved? You were helping your mom hang up curtains? And kind of dancing on a chair with the music blasting?"

The dancing part sounded right. The first night in the new house, my mom and I had turned the radio up loud while unpacking . . . and we'd had the windows open to air out some paint fumes. But it had been dark by then, and I hadn't seen Patrick at all, or even really thought about the obvious fact that anybody walking past on the sidewalk would have seen me dancing on a chair like an idiot.

"You did this scuba diver move." Okay, now I really wanted to die. I knew the exact one he meant. It was this cheesy dance move I used to do with my best friend in first grade. You kind of pinched your nose with one hand and wiggled your body like you were going underwater. My mom and I had been listening to "Yellow Submarine" by the Beatles at the time. "You smiled, and I was pretty sure you waved back, so I thought you recognized me at the mall yesterday. I could have sworn you did."

I shook my head.

"Sorry! I probably should have come over to say hi and introduce myself as your neighbor, just in case, but my break was almost up." He looked more than a little uncomfortable, like maybe he *had* wanted to talk to me yesterday at the store, but hadn't been able to work up the nerve. "Anyway . . . it's nice to formally meet you." He extended a mittened hand. "Small world, right?"

I bit at my lip, returning his handshake. Unfortunately, where Patrick was concerned, the world seemed to be much, much, much too small. And then, partly because my eyes were going to freeze open if I kept staring at him in disbelief, and partly because I didn't know what else to do, I walked around to the driver's side of the car and got in.

Chapter 4

"Where exactly are we going?" I asked for the third time as I turned my head left and right, then checked my rear-view mirror before executing a cautious right turn into a totally empty intersection.

"Just drive straight for a while," Patrick answered. "I'll know it when I see it." He stared out the passenger-side window, barely seeming concerned about the fact that his life was in grave danger. Come to think of it, he hadn't even acted worried when, after helping me to adjust the side mirrors and seat back, I'd asked him which pedal was the brake and which was the gas. I mean, obviously, I knew the gas was on the right side in our car, but when you were driving an unfamiliar vehicle you could never be too careful about these things.

"Go left at the next stop sign," Patrick instructed. "You're doing great."

I wasn't, actually. I'd already nearly given us both whiplash when I'd slammed on the brakes halfway down our street. I'd been testing to make sure they worked well on the icy road conditions (they did), but in retrospect I probably should have warned Patrick first.

"So," I started, hoping some small talk would calm me down. I was gripping the wheel so tightly my knuckles were white—first because I was driving, but also because I was still in shock that pen-buying, tooth-checking, Dina's-crush guy was my new driving instructor *and* neighbor. So much for my plan to avoid him. "How long have you and your grandparents been living on Gamble Avenue?"

"It's just me and my grandpa now," Patrick answered. "He's been there forever. My great-grandparents were the original owners of the house. It's one of the oldest in the area. They built it themselves in 1910, way before all the prefab houses started popping up around it, or any shopping malls were nearby. My great-grandpa even built the house you and your mom just bought." My ears perked up. So that explained why our new house looked so much like Mr. Connor's—and why they were the only two older homes on a block full of cookie-cutter houses with two-car garages. "Then my grandparents eventually divided up the land and sold it. But I'm telling you a million things you probably don't care about," he apologized. "Sometimes I talk too much. Sorry." I didn't actually mind, especially since the more he talked, the less I had to participate in the conversation—which was a good thing, since I was concentrating pretty hard on not getting us killed. "You wanted to know when I moved here," he went on. "My grandma died in November from a stroke. I just moved down from Toronto to help my grandpa out around the house. I'm finishing high school here."

"Really? You left all your friends behind and everything? That's nice of you."

He shrugged like it was no big deal. "Not really. I mean, I only have a semester of high school left. I figured everyone would be going their separate ways soon, anyway. I keep in touch with a bunch of friends back home. Plus, I'd do anything for my grandpa. I like helping him out and keeping him company. But I have selfish motives, too." He took his gloves off and rubbed his hands together to warm them. Even though it felt like we'd been driving forever, the heater hadn't quite kicked in yet. "He gets all the good cable channels. And instead of complaining that I play my music too loud, he just shuts off his hearing aid. He never gets upset about anything." Patrick started fiddling with the heating vent flap things, turning them all to blow in my direction. "Stop!" he said, looking up all of a sudden. My heart leaped up and I slammed on the brakes, throwing us both forward against our seat belts.

"Oof." He rubbed at his chest.

"Sorry!" I squeaked, making a pained face. First I'd accused him of stalking me in a parking lot, and now I'd nearly given him whiplash for the second time in half an hour. I was clearly off to a wicked awesome start getting to know my new neighbor.

"No. My fault," he apologized. "I got so busy talking, I forgot you're nervous on the roads. I should have used a calmer voice. I just meant, 'You can stop now. We're here.'"

"We're where?"

"Here. The place where we're going."

I looked around, my heart continuing to beat loudly against my ribs. We were in old Middleford, on Carlton, six blocks from where my mom and I used to live. It was a street full of big, old trees and expensive, historic, three-story houses.

"See that car?" Patrick asked. It was a red convertible parked at the side of the road. "Pretty nice, right?" I nodded, still trying to catch my breath. "That's an Audi A4. It'd run you somewhere around forty thousand dollars. Why anyone would drive a convertible in the winter, I have no idea, but some people are idiots."

I gave him a weird look. I definitely didn't have $40,000. And I didn't need to learn about buying a luxury car. I just needed to learn about driving a regular one. "And see that one?" He pointed to the one in front. "It's a BMW 7-Series. You're looking at eighty thousand, minimum."

"That's nice," I said.

"You think so?" he asked. "I always thought they were kind of squashed looking. And my friend's dad back in Canada has one. He says they guzzle gas. Personally, when this one dies, and I graduate and get a decent job, I'm buying a hybrid." We sat in silence for a few seconds.

"Okay, now what?" I asked.

"Now you parallel park between those two cars." I must have given him a look like he had banana trees growing out his ears, because he started laughing.

"You can't be serious," I said. "Shouldn't we be practicing this in, like, a deserted parking lot somewhere? Plus, you just told me that those two cars combined cost at least a hundred and twenty thousand dollars. You *do* realize my mom and I don't have that kind of cash, right? How do you expect me to pay when I total them?"

"You're not going to total them."

I let my head fall forward against the steering wheel and shut my eyes. "Okay, Patrick, you've obviously never driven with me before. If you had, you'd know that there's no point sitting here discussing this. I can't do it."

"I've been driving with you for the past half hour," he answered. "That's how I know that you can." I obviously didn't look convinced. "There won't be a scratch on those cars when you're finished. I promise. I'm going to be right here beside you, helping." I sighed. "Parallel parking is like riding a bike—" he started.

I cut him off. "The last time I rode a bike I broke my ankle and came this close to killing some lady's cat."

"Okay." He paused. "It's like learning to swim—"

"I sink."

"Okay. What *can* you do?"

I sighed again. "I read. I bake cookies and cakes. I

study. I pretty much excel at all things safe and boring that involve sitting at home and *not* parallel parking between a hundred and twenty thousand dollars worth of cars."

"Baking!" he said. "Parallel parking is exactly like baking." I was *not* going to be parallel parking in that spot. No way, no how. But I had to hear this. "You've got your ingredients, right?" I could tell his mind was racing. "The car and the spot. And you've got your recipe. Here. Pull up beside the BMW. Not too close. About two feet away. Line the bumpers up, then put on your turn signal."

"Patrick. That's a really bad idea. I don't think you understand. . . ."

"Here," he said, ignoring me. "Give it a tiny bit of gas."

"No way."

"Just try." Against my better judgment, I gave in and Patrick guided the wheel as I pressed gently on the gas pedal. We pulled alongside the BMW. "Okay. So you take one car." He pointed at the steering wheel. "Check!" I was trying not to hyperventilate. "You take two feet of space." He rolled down his window and leaned out, letting in a gush of cold air. "Check!" He motioned for me to take the wheel again. "You put it in reverse." He adjusted the gear shift for me. "Then use juuuust a little gas, and you stir it all the way to the right. Stir," he said, and I wrenched the wheel around, feeling like I was about to barf. The car inched back. "Stir stir stir stir. Good. Okay. Brake." I stepped on the pedal. Hard. We both lurched forward. Again. "Okay. Good. We'll work on smooth braking later."

I pulled my hat off and shoved it between the seats. I could feel my forehead sweating, and I was sure I had a brutal case of hat head, but I didn't care. I was so mad at Patrick for making me do this. I didn't have anything to prove to him, and I didn't care how bad I looked.

"Okay, now just a little bit of gas again and stir it to the left. Keep looking over your shoulder to watch where you're going." I wrenched the wheel around, swearing under my breath. "Okay, brake." I did, more gently this time. "There. Now just pull forward and center the car, like you're sliding a cookie sheet into the oven. You want at least two feet of space at the front and back, and about half a foot from the curb." I pulled forward, hit the brake again, put the car in park, and shut off the ignition.

"See?" he said, grinning. "I knew you could do it. And that was, like, extreme parallel parking. Now that you've parked between two cars that cost more than your entire university education will, you'll never be scared again." He held up his hand for a high five.

I did *not* high-five him back. Instead, I unbuckled my seat belt and got out, slamming the door behind me. Patrick got out, too.

"Check it out." He walked around the car. "You're exactly half a foot from the curb. *Exactly.* Honestly, I kind of want to take a picture of this parallel park and frame it, because *that's* how perfect it is. It's like the *Mona Lisa* of parallel parks, or something."

I was fuming too much to listen. It was a miracle I'd made it into the space without damaging $120,000 worth of luxury cars. He was an idiot if he thought there was any other explanation. And I was an idiot for letting him talk me into doing something so risky. If I'd hit those cars, we never would have been able to pay for the damages—even with Patrick's insurance coverage. My mom and I would have probably had to sell our new, cheaper house. We'd be on the streets, sleeping next to Jack the homeless guy and kicking ice chips at strangers who wouldn't give us their bus money. I walked past him, opened the passenger-side door, got in, and slammed it shut.

"Hey!" Patrick knocked on the window but I refused to look at him. My hands were shaking in my lap. I wiped some sweat off my forehead and blinked back tears. He knocked again. This time I rolled the window down a crack. "What are you doing?" he asked.

"You're driving," I said, then looked straight ahead again. He came around to the driver's side and got in. Neither of us said a single word the whole way home.

"You working tomorrow?" Patrick asked finally as he effortlessly backed the car into the driveway of his grandfather's house.

"Noon to four," I answered, unbuckling my seat belt.

"I'm off at three thirty," he said. "I'll wait for you. You can practice driving home. We're going the same way, anyway. Makes sense, right?" It did. But just because it made sense, didn't mean I wanted to do it.

"What've we got left? Thirteen days before your road test? There's no way you're failing this time. You're an awesome driver, Elyse. You just need to work on your confidence."

I knew he was trying to help, that he was trying to be nice. So why was it that I couldn't seem to keep the sarcastic tone out of my voice? "Right," I said, closing the car door and walking away. "Because I'm the Leonardo da Vinci of left-hand turns." I didn't look back, but I'd swear I heard him laughing at me softly as I trudged up the path to my front door.

I kicked off my boots and glanced at the clock on the DVD player. It was 7:10, plus our car was in the driveway, so I knew my mom was home. "Hello?" I called. Nobody answered. There weren't any cooking smells coming from the kitchen. "You won't believe what the neighbor made me do." I started telling the story, figuring my mom was just in the bathroom and would hear me through the door. "I seriously think we should cancel these driving lessons before something goes horribly wrong." Still no answer. "Hello?" I stuck my head up the stairwell. And that was when I heard it: a faint banging noise. It got louder as I walked toward the kitchen, but there was nobody there. I opened the door to the basement.

"Elyse?!" The banging resumed. "Elyse?!" My mother's voice was muffled, but I didn't miss the hint of panic in it. "Elyse, come help me." I flew down the stairs, taking them two at a time. It took a few seconds for my eyes to adjust to the dim light, but when they did I gasped. The huge, heavy wooden wardrobe my mom had been sanding to keep our extra winter coats in was lying facedown on the cement floor—its doors open. A single hand—my mother's—was reaching out from underneath a small gap between the floor and the wardrobe, waving frantically for my attention. I knelt down on the ground. "Oh my God. Are you okay? Are you crushed? Do you need an ambulance? Mom, can you breathe? I'm calling 911." I raced toward the stairs, my knees trembling.

"Elyse, I'm fine." Was my mother laughing or crying? I couldn't tell for sure without seeing her face. She gestured with her single visible hand, telling the story just like she would have if she weren't underneath a 200-pound wardrobe. "I had a few minutes when I got home, so I thought I'd sand the insides of the doors before making dinner. I stood up on the shelf to reach the top and the whole thing tipped on me. I've been trying to bang my way through the back panel, but it's no use. Can you lift up the wardrobe, sweetie? Just a little? Get the cement block that's in the corner under the bag of peat moss. Prop it underneath and I should be able to crawl out."

I got the cinder block she was talking about and somehow managed to heave the wardrobe up several inches. I pushed the big cement brick under with my foot, fighting back tears the whole time. A second later, my mother shimmied out from underneath, stood up, and brushed the floor dirt and sawdust out of her hair. She crouched down to examine the wardrobe. One of the doors had cracked a bit in the fall and, even with the two of us lifting, there was no way we'd ever be able to get it standing upright again. The thing weighed a ton.

"Well, maybe we could just store our extra winter coats in plastic bins under the stairs instead," she said, and that was when my mother noticed the tears streaming down my face. She understood immediately. "Oh, Elyse. Oh, sweetie. I'm all right." She stood up and held out her arms to show me. "Not a scratch. I'm fine."

"But what if you hadn't been? Mom, that thing could have crushed you."

"But it didn't." She put her arms around me, then pulled away to wipe the tears off my cheeks with her fingers.

"And you were all alone down there. What if I hadn't come right home for some reason?"

"But you did."

"I was supposed to help you sand this last night," I sniffed, looking at the wardrobe, "when I was done studying. I forgot. If I hadn't forgotten, you wouldn't have been doing it all by yourself."

"That's all right, Elyse. It's my responsibility to get these things done. I'm the adult in this family." I hated it when she said things like that. Maybe it was true when I was a kid, but now I was seventeen. She shouldn't have to take care of everything all on her own anymore. It was bad enough that my father had walked out on her with barely a backward glance; she should have at least been able to count on me. "From now on I'll be more careful when I'm fixing things around the house. I promise," she said.

"And ask me for help," I said, giving her my best "I am so serious right now" look, which she totally ignored.

"Come on," she said instead. "Come upstairs. We'll order a pizza. You'll feel better after you've had something to eat. Then you can help me with my homework assignment."

My mom's "homework assignment" turned out to be hand-lettering forty-five place cards using gold ink and a calligraphy pen. After an afternoon of extreme parallel parking followed by the near-crushing-death-of-my-mother-by-a-wardrobe, my hand wasn't exactly steady, to say the least. I went through five different cards before I finally did one that was good enough to keep.

"They've got the Bradford ballroom booked out for lunch, and they're closing the entire spa for the afternoon," my mom explained. "The whole thing is being catered by Chez Pierre, and they're giving away all kinds of raffle prizes." She stacked another neatly lettered card onto her pile. "I still miss Chudleigh's Auto Insurance, but I have to say, they never had staff appreciation days like this."

I took a bite of my Hawaiian slice and washed it down with some iced tea while I watched my mother work. The bags under her eyes were huge and dark, but besides that, she looked good. She'd been waking up at six A.M. the past two days so she'd have time to blow-dry her hair and do her makeup. Apparently one of the requirements of working reception at a spa was to look put-together. She even had pink polish on her nails—something I'd never seen her wear before. She noticed me noticing it. "Oh, Claire—one of the aestheticians—did this for me at break. It doesn't look too glitzy, does it?"

I smiled, putting down my pizza crust. "It's nice," I said. I wiped my hands on my napkin and picked up another place card to letter. "Seriously?" I looked down at the list of names my mom had given me. "This is somebody's real name?" My mother finished clearing the plates, then peered over my shoulder.

"Oh. Valter. He's the spa's Swedish masseuse."

"And his last name's Bigaskis?"

"Yes."

"Pronounced 'big-ass-kiss'?" I asked, enunciating the word in my best imitation of a Swedish accent. "Like, 'Valter Big-ass-kiss'?"

"Elyse," my mother scolded in the same tone she used to use when I'd pick my nose or make farting sounds with my male cousins as a kid. "That's not funny."

"Yes it is," I said. "Kind of, at least. You've got to admit." But my mother didn't look like she was about to admit anything. "Val-ter Big-ass-kiss," I said again, giggling a little to myself as I lettered the place card. My mom hadn't cracked a smile, so I tried to stop laughing.

"Oh." She sat down and picked up another place card, changing the subject. "Dina called for you earlier. I guess she didn't realize you had a driving lesson. She was wondering if she could confirm you for the chocolate-vanilla cheesecake. Sounds like a fun party."

I groaned. It had been a long day. The last thing I wanted to think about was Valentine's Day, or Dina's ridiculous party, but now that Dina had told my mother all about it, I knew there was no way out—I'd be going.

"I told her no problem. I'll help you bake it if you want. We still have your stuffed panda bear collection, too. I packed them in one of those filing boxes for the move. It's somewhere in the basement. I said we'd see if we could dig them up. They'd make great decorations."

"Mom!" I cried. It was bad enough that I was being forced to party on Valentine's Day when all I wanted to do was mope. I didn't want to drag along a bunch of stupid childhood stuffed animals.

"You'll have fun, Elyse. It's good that you're going out."

I sighed. "And it's two weeks from today, too. You know what that means, don't you?" I gave her a blank look. "You'll have passed your road test by then. You can drive to Dina's yourself."

I dropped Valter Bigaskis's finished name card into my pile and reached for another. *Drew Hulse*. Nothing funny about that one. In fact, it was one of the most depressing names I'd ever heard, which was fitting, because I was suddenly feeling gloomy—not to mention very, very tired.

Chapter 5

On Saturday morning my bootlace came untied just as I was running down the steps. I stopped to tie it and, as a result, just missed the stupid number four bus again. Since my mom had already left for the grocery store, I had no choice but to wait. I ended up being fifteen minutes late for work. When I got there, Dina was wrestling with a bunch of unruly helium balloons while trying to sell a frazzled-looking mother on the customer loyalty Cupid promotion.

"Thanks," the mother was saying distractedly, keeping an eye on her two sons, who were playing tag dangerously close to the crystal dolphin figurines. "But it's my son's sixth birthday party today. We'll get enough noisy, battery powered toys as it is."

The day before, when someone had shared a similar concern, I'd overheard Dina trying to convince them that—if you took the batteries out—Cupid could also make a lovely centerpiece for a Valentine's Day dinner table, but for some reason, she didn't even bother. "Dammit," she said instead, under her breath, as a robot-shaped foil balloon made a break for freedom and floated toward the ceiling.

"I'll get the stepladder," I offered, dumping my bag behind the counter and heading for the back room. As soon as the mother had left with her bratty kids and her bunch of balloons, I turned to Dina. "You don't seem so good. Everything okay?"

She sank down miserably on the stool behind the counter. "Elyse, if you called somebody, and they said they'd call you right back, when would you expect to hear from them?"

"I don't know," I said. "Maybe in a couple of minutes." I could tell from the look on her face that I hadn't given the answer she'd been hoping for. "Or, it depends. If they're really busy with something, it might be longer."

"How much longer?"

"An hour, maybe? Two hours."

"Not sixteen?"

I wasn't a hundred percent sure what we were talking about, although I had a pretty good guess. "No. Probably not sixteen." I hesitated. "Unless something really important came up. Or there was an emergency."

"Oh my God. I thought of that, but then I tried to talk myself out of it. But what if you're right? I called Damien right after work yesterday. Ten after six. He was just on his way out and he sounded *really* out of breath. He said he'd call me right back but I haven't heard anything. And I've texted him twice since then. Oh my God. It all makes sense, though. What if one of his parents fell down the stairs or had a heart attack or something? And then he had to rush home? Maybe he's at Middleford General right now? Should I text him again? No, wait. You can't use cell phones in a hospital, right? Because of the heart monitors. Elyse, do you think I should call his parents' house to make sure everything's okay?"

"I'm sure everything's fine, Dina," I said. "And if it isn't, then he's probably just too busy to call right now."

"You're right," she said, clearly unconvinced but seeming like she wanted to believe me. "I'll just wait. He'll get in touch if he needs me, right?"

"Of course he will."

She pulled her cell phone out of her back pocket and flipped it open, just to make sure it was still working, then put it away before walking toward the card aisle to help an old lady with a cane. While I was ringing through the old lady's anniversary card, I saw Dina check her phone again. Suddenly, I thought of the perfect way to distract her.

"I have something to tell you," I said as soon as the store was quiet again. "You're not going to believe it, but guess who my new driving instructor *and* neighbor is . . ."

"You're kidding!" Dina said once I'd told her the whole story. "That's such a coincidence. He seemed so nice. Is he a good teacher?" she asked.

"The worst." I told her my parallel parking horror story from the night before. She was appropriately sympathetic. I was just about to tell her the stuff I'd found out about him moving here to take care of his grandfather (which I knew she'd go gaga over), but Dina's back pocket started buzzing. "It's Damien," she said. She slid out her phone, flipped it open, and read the text message.

"Everything okay?"

"Yeah." She scrolled through his message a second time. "That's a relief," she added, but she sounded disappointed. "He was at a keg party with some friends, got drunk, crashed there, and just woke up. He forgot I called."

She started pressing buttons.

"Please tell me you're not texting him back this second." She looked up. "The guy didn't even apologize for taking sixteen hours to get back to you. It didn't even cross his mind that you might have been upset or worried."

She paused, lowering the phone. "You think I should wait?"

"Yes!" I said. "And, anyway, you just answered your phone while I was talking to you and rudely interrupted my story about pen-buying guy—I mean, Patrick." She looked up. "I was going to tell you how he was asking about you in the car." It wasn't that I was intending to be dishonest with her . . . but the lie just kind of slipped out.

"No way," she said. "He wasn't! What did he want to know?"

"Well . . ." I stalled for time while I tried to think up something that sounded vague enough not to get me busted, but specific enough to seem true. "He wanted to know how long you'd been working here and, um—what your hobbies were."

"What did you tell him?"

"I told him you'd been working for Mr. Goodman since the summer, and that you were really into supporting important causes in your spare time. And it turns out he's all about helping people and putting others first, too." I soothed my conscience by adding that last part, because he'd definitely said something about helping his grandfather out around the house, anyway. She flipped the phone shut. "I also mentioned the panda party," I went on, improvising.

"What did he say?"

"Not much, but I think it's just because he's too nice to ask for an invitation. I'm pretty sure he'd say yes if you asked him yourself."

"Really? Is he single?"

"I don't know." He hadn't mentioned a girlfriend but, then again, we'd only spent an hour together, and in the last twenty minutes, I'd been too mad to talk to him. It was possible he had a girlfriend, either here or else back in Toronto.

"Can you find out?"

"We have another lesson this afternoon. I'll see what I can do."

"Oh my God," Dina said. "Maybe this is, like, fate. I mean, he walks into the store and we meet, and then he ends up being your neighbor *and* your driving instructor, so I've totally got an in." She slid her phone into her back pocket.

Mission accomplished. "So you're not texting Damien back now?"

"No." She smiled, then added defiantly, "I'm busy at work. He can wait a while, right?"

I stepped out from behind the cash so she could take over. "Dina, as far as I'm concerned, that jerkwad can wait forever."

"Elyse!" she said, covering Cupid's ears with her hands. "Watch your language in front of the baby!" But she was smiling, so there was no question in my mind that I'd done the right thing. Even if I'd had to tell a few small, white lies, the ends totally justified the means.

Or, at least, that's what I thought until three thirty, when Patrick walked into the store. I was stuck with a customer who wanted to know every little difference between the four brands of white copier paper we carried, but Dina waved him over. By the time I managed to get my butt over to the cash, they were already talking pandas. Things were about to get kind of complicated.

"So I think it's important," Dina was saying. "If we can raise just five hundred dollars we'll make a small but real difference in helping to preserve the population of giant pandas. And, like I'm sure Elyse told you, the whole theme is going to be black and white, so it'll be really fun." Patrick shot me a strange look but, to his credit, didn't mention that this was the first he'd heard about a panda party. "Elyse is going to be baking some snacks. And, trust me, you don't want to miss her cheesecake. So, if you're free . . ." She trailed off.

"Yeah," he said, giving me the weird look again. "I think I might be."

"Cool." Her eyes lit up. "Hang on. Just let me ring this up and then I'll tell you all about Oreo—the panda we're adopting. I can even show you a picture. Talk about cute!" Patrick politely stepped aside as the paper guy piled six packages of EverTree brand copier stock on the cash.

"What are you doing here so early?" I asked while Dina rang up the purchase and bagged the paper. My irritation about the driving lesson was still pretty fresh. "I'm not done until four. And you can't just hang out here. Sometimes Mr. Goodman stops in on weekends."

"Who said I was hanging out? I'm shopping." He picked up a Beanie Baby rabbit and shook its head, flopping its ears around.

"Oh yeah? For a bunny?"

"Nah," he said, setting the Beanie Baby down. "No bunnies today. I need a pen."

"You just got one yesterday."

"Yeah. About that?" He ran his fingers through his curls. "It's a little too sploodgy."

"Sploodgy?" I raised my eyebrows.

"Yeah. Like, when you press down on the tip, the ink sploodges out. Do you have anything that writes really crisply?"

"Right," I said, trying to keep the mocking tone out of my voice. "Something crisp, not sploodgy. Follow me."

Patrick took ages in the pen aisle, doodling with

different pens on the scraps of notepaper Mr. Goodman left out for that reason. "This one is pretty good," he said finally, holding up a WriteSmart ballpoint. "But do you have it in black?" I searched through the bin and thrust a black pen toward him.

"Here."

"Whoa," he said, jumping back a bit. "Getting hostile with the writing instruments there. You're not still mad about that parallel parking thing, are you?" he asked, taking the pen from me carefully, like I might have laced it with explosives.

"Mad? Why would I be mad?" I shot back.

"I don't know," he said. "Maybe because I was kind of a jerk about it." That took me off guard. He tucked his new pen behind his ear. "I've been thinking about it, and look, I knew you weren't going to hit those cars. But that doesn't mean you felt ready, I guess. Like you said, we probably should have practiced in a parking lot or something first. I'm sorry. Okay? I won't do anything like that again."

"Okay," I said, my anger melting away so suddenly that I didn't know what to say or do next. Why had I been so pissed off in the first place? I already almost couldn't remember. "Um. Anyway," I stuttered. "I've got stuff to finish shelving, but Dina can ring that up for you at the cash."

"Okay. But, wait." He stopped me. "Can you help me with one more thing first?"

"Yeah?"

"I need to buy a valentine." Now it was his turn to look embarrassed.

"For your girlfriend?" Maybe I could get the dirt Dina was looking for.

"Not exactly." His cheeks went kind of red, making his freckles stand out. "Not yet, anyway. Just this girl I met." I glanced ever-so-quickly in Dina's direction to see if he'd follow my gaze, but he was busy staring at the floor.

"Well," I started, "we have a big selection." I led him over to the valentine section, which was marked by an absolutely giant, obscenely sparkly heart-shaped sign hanging from the ceiling. LOVE IS IN THE AIR. "This is where the romance happens." I pointed to the sign, rolling my eyes. "In my personal opinion, almost everything in this section is nauseating, but a lot of girls like this kind of thing."

I picked up a card with Tweetie bird on the front. I opened it and read: "I'm lucky to have a tweetheart like you, who's caring and loving and wonderful, too." I stuffed it back in the slot. "Tweetheart isn't even a real word."

I picked up another with a pastel-colored painting of a couple dancing on the front. The woman was in a flowing red gown. "My dear, my heart, my lady in red. When I'm with you, I feel inspir-ed. Happy Valentine's." I closed the card and made a face. "Really? Since when has the word 'red' rhymed with the word 'inspired'? Since never. But that's what you'll find in half these cards. It's like the companies can't afford to hire poets who know how to rhyme anymore. Sad."

Patrick was smiling. "Well, what about this one? Girls would think this is cute, right?" He handed me a card with a picture of a baby riding a motorcycle.

"Baby, you get my engine going." I handed it back. "Okay, first of all. Gross. Not cute. And, second, the joke card is a huge cop-out. It's like you're saying, 'I really like you, but I'm too much of a chicken to actually come out and say it, so I'm giving you this picture of a baby in a motorcycle helmet instead.' Again, kinda sad."

"You know you're not the world's greatest salesperson, right?" he teased, putting the card back.

"Hey," I retorted. "I'm trying to do you a favor here." I picked out a card with a simple red heart on the front, set against a silver backdrop. "This is the least bad one we have." I handed it to him and watched him open it.

"It's blank," he observed.

"Exactly," I said. "If you like someone, you should care enough to write your own message. Or, at least, that's what I've always thought."

He flipped the card over to check the price, then put it back. "I'll think about that one," he said.

Dina had finished with the paper guy and was holding the picture of Oreo, the panda, in the air to get Patrick's attention. He gave her a little wave to let her know he'd be there in a sec.

"On the other hand, though," I added quickly. "Some girls are really into the corny stuff." I hoped he'd get my drift. "We just got this adorable one with puppies wearing floppy hats. Dina, for example, loves it." That was an understatement. She'd practically melted into a puddle of goo the first time she'd seen it. "I can show it to you tomorrow. But right now you'd better go meet the bear," I said.

"Right," he answered, "and pay for this." He slid the nonsploodgy pen out from behind his ear and turned to go.

"Hey!" I called, getting his attention. He stopped. "Do me a favor, okay? Don't promise Dina you'll go to her party unless you really mean it."

"Why wouldn't I mean it?" he asked.

"I don't know." I thought of the girl he wanted to buy a valentine for—his "not exactly girlfriend." If it wasn't Dina he was talking about, I didn't want him leading her on. She was way too sensitive for that kind of thing. "It just means a lot to her, okay? So if you say you're going, then show up."

"Oh, I'll be there," he said. "Black-and-white snacks? Endangered species bingo? Are you kidding me? It's gonna be awesome. Ever since you told me *all about it* yesterday, I've been counting down the days."

I gave him my best apologetic look. "About that . . ." I started, but he seemed to have already let the subject drop.

"Don't worry," he continued. "I'm going. Wouldn't miss it. It's gonna be total panda-monium." I rolled my eyes at his stupid joke, but there was something in his tone that put me at ease. There was no question in my mind: Patrick might be annoying, but he was mostly a decent guy. I could tell that he meant what he said.

Chapter 6

True to his word, Patrick didn't push me as hard in our driving lesson that afternoon. In fact, there was no parallel parking at all. He *did* make me drive one exit on the highway (something that made my pulse race even faster than parking), but even that wasn't completely disastrous. I must have checked my blind spot ten times, but somehow I managed to merge before the dotted lines on the road ran out.

It also kind of helped that, as soon as we got in the car, Patrick took a CD out of the glove box and slid it into the player. "Surely Sarah," he said as the music started. It was kind of mellow, with a lot of guitar and hardly any drums. "Do you know them?"

I shook my head. When I'd been dating Matt, he'd taken me to a few heavy metal concerts. The singers were always dressed in black. They wore silver chains hanging from their pockets, jumped up and down, and shouted a lot. For some reason, I'd felt like I had to pretend that I thought it was totally hardcore and awesome. But I was really more into classic rock. Stuff like Van Morrison and the Doors, which my uncle Tom (who played the bass in an amateur, old-guy rock band) had introduced me to. Besides that, the only thing I really listened to (and not by choice) was the soft rock, seventy-percent-Céline-Dion radio station my mom always had on.

"You should give them a try," Patrick said, turning up the volume. "I think you'd really like them." To my surprise, I *did* like them. The melody was pretty, and kind of catchy and, without even realizing what I was doing, I released my death grip on the steering wheel and started drumming my fingers along to the music. By the time we were done with the lesson, I was so relaxed that I actually made the left-hand turn onto our street (across two lanes of traffic) without any cars honking their horns at me from behind for taking too long.

It would have been a not-so-bad lesson all around, actually, if Patrick hadn't wanted me to practice backing into his grandfather's driveway. "It's pretty easy. Line the rear bumper up with the edge of the driveway," he instructed.

I'll admit: I knew my wheels were crooked, but I was hungry. My mom always made a roast chicken after she grocery shopped on Saturdays, and I could practically taste it already, so I didn't bother pulling forward to fix them. Twisting my body around to see over my shoulder, I hit the gas pedal and came into the driveway at a 45-degree angle, landing the front wheels in the garden between our houses and slamming on the brakes with the back bumper sitting about two feet from Patrick's garage. It maybe wouldn't have mattered, except for the crunching sound we heard as I backed up. An innocent shrub in Patrick's side of the front garden had obviously paid the price for my impatience.

"Oh God," I said, getting out of the car to examine the flattened collection of twigs. "I'm so sorry. I'll buy your grandfather a new one as soon as the garden center opens, I promise."

Patrick drew in a breath as he crouched down and gently lifted one of the crushed branches. He let it drop into the snow again. "Thanks, but I don't think this one can be replaced. It's a blossoming Japanese cherry bush. They're kind of rare."

I felt like I was going to cry. Leave it to me to run over the most rare and beautiful bush on the entire block. "Well, maybe I can order one off the internet, or something. Somebody must import them. I'll find one. I swear. *I told you* I sucked at backing in." I looked at the mangled mass of twigs again and sighed. This clearly wasn't Patrick's fault. "God, I'm an idiot. I knew I didn't have the right angle. I should have pulled forward and straightened out the wheels, but I was in a rush. I'm really, really sorry."

Patrick stood up, a smile breaking across his face as he laid a hand on my coat sleeve. "Elyse, relax. I was kidding," he confessed. "But, by the way, you're right. You just needed to pull forward a bit to straighten your wheels. Besides that, you were doing great. It's not a blossoming Japanese cherry bush." I froze, then pulled my arm away. "It's some kind of super weed. We have them all over the backyard, too. They smell like feet and get these wicked spikes on them in the summer. You can run it over again if you want."

I stared at him in shock. I couldn't *believe* he'd done that to me How was it possible for somebody to be so nice at times and so aggravating at others?

"Oh man," he said, catching my look. "You're mad at me again." He pulled his hat down over his eyes, then pulled it up a little, peeking out at me, trying to be cute. "You hate me. *Again*. I shouldn't have said that. It's just that, you looked so serious. I *had* to tease you. Okay. *I'm* the one who's an idiot."

I didn't disagree.

"See you tomorrow," I said instead, giving him a small, tight smile. We were at T-minus twelve days to my driving test. I needed him, and there was no use being mad all the time, even if he was mostly infuriating. "And, thanks for the lesson," I added, rather generously I thought. "It wasn't totally horrible."

He nodded. "I'll take that as a compliment, I guess. And, hey, next time, if you straighten the wheels, you'll nail it. Then you'll be, like, the Baryshnikov of backing in."

I turned my back so he wouldn't see me smiling for real and headed toward my house. "Hey, wait," he said.

I stopped, one foot deep in the snowbank between our driveways. "About this panda party. You going with anyone?"

It either said something about my total lack of interest in dating, or the fact that my nerves were still a little shot from the rare Japanese shrub incident . . . but I didn't even understand the question. "Depends if I pass my road test. I'm still betting it's a fifty-fifty chance I'll fail—no offense to your teaching skills. I might get my mom to drive me."

"No. I mean, *going with someone*. Like, your boyfriend?"

I actually laughed. "Uh-uh. I mean. No. I don't have a boyfriend. I'm not going out with anyone. But I'm sure you can bring someone if you want." I hesitated, knowing that if he showed up with some other girl it would ruin Dina's entire Valentine's Day. "But, then again, Dina will probably need a lot of help setting up and everything. If you didn't bring a date, then maybe you could help out more."

"Sure," he said. "Yeah, no problem. I'm not going out with anyone either. And I'm good at pouring chips into bowls and putting up streamers and stuff." He leaned down and picked up a mitten full of snow, formed it into a ball, and threw it softly against his grandfather's garage door. "How come you don't have a boyfriend?" he asked, reaching down to pick up some more snow. "Is your mom really strict or something?"

"No." I wiggled my toes inside my boots to keep them warm. "No, trust me. My mom would love it if I was going out with someone. She thinks I study too much. I don't date because . . ." I trailed off. I'd known Patrick all of three days. He didn't need to hear the gory details of the Matt Love heartbreak. "It's complicated," I finished. "Or, no. Wait. It's not complicated at all. Men are pigs." I realized a second too late that I'd just insulted his entire half of our species. "High school guys, especially. I mean, not all of them. Obviously. But ninety-eight percent."

"Is that a scientific fact?" he asked.

"Pretty much," I answered.

"Well, what about the other two percent?"

"The other two percent are really hard to find."

"They do exist though," he countered.

"Right," I said sarcastically, then I stepped out of the snowbank and lifted a branch of the totally smushed, totally not-rare spike-weed with the toe of my boot. "I'll believe that when I actually meet one."

I had Sunday off, so my mom and I spent the day unpacking the last of our boxes. It was nice—if a little weird—to see all of our books lined up on the built-in shelves, our photos on the new mantelpiece. Even though the house was smaller than our last house—with hardwood floors that creaked and groaned, cracking plaster, and old-fashioned windows that let in a draft—it was starting to seem more like home.

"Look at this," my mom said, coming down the hallway. She was holding something curled in the palm of her hand. "I found it between the floorboards in the attic while I was putting the boxes away." I set the towels I'd been folding on the linen closet shelf and went to see. It was a thin, tarnished chain with a tiny pendant on it. "I think it's an opal," my mom said, tipping the small, iridescent blue stone in the light. It was shaped like a heart. "Must have belonged to the old owners. But they didn't leave a forwarding address. It's yours now if you want it." She opened my fingers and dropped the necklace into my hand. "There's some silver polish under the sink."

I didn't usually wear jewelry—especially cheesy heart-shaped stuff—but there was something kind of sweet and simple about the necklace that made me not hate it. I dropped it into my pocket, planning to clean it up later.

My mom ducked into her bedroom and came out dragging the laundry hamper behind her. "I'm going to put in a load before I start painting the bathroom," she said. "Do you have anything you want washed?"

"No," I said. "Not really." My mom started off down the hallway with the heavy hamper, and that's when I noticed the dust in her hair from the attic; the tired slump of her shoulders. We'd mostly been in separate rooms so I wasn't certain, but I couldn't remember seeing her stop all day to eat anything, or to sit down. And I was positive she hadn't gotten around to showering yet.

"Hey, Mom," I said. "Why don't you leave the bathroom? We can live with puke green for one more day." It was hard to understand why anyone had picked that color for a bathroom in the first place. It made everyone who went in there look like they were just getting over the stomach flu. "We could rent a movie. Something brainless, like a romantic comedy. Make some popcorn. Take a break for tonight."

"*You* want to rent a romantic comedy?" my mom asked, raising her eyebrows doubtfully. I didn't want to, actually. I hated the whole "boy meets girl, they fall in love but—oh—they can't possibly be together because of some terrible but really very easy-to-resolve misunderstanding" plots that always ended happily ever after with a passionate kiss and/or a wedding, but I knew they were my mom's favorites so . . .

"Yeah. I do," I said.

"Hang on." She was grinning. "I'll put this laundry in, run a brush through my hair, and grab the car keys. There's a Video 411 at Carson Square."

Big mistake. An hour later, I was in sappy story heartbreak hell. "Oh, I can't look," my mom said, covering her eyes. "He's going to see the other girl from behind, wearing the same sweater, and think it's his fiancée. And they made such a cute couple, too. Didn't you think it was romantic when he had the airplane skywrite his marriage proposal?"

I thought it was kind of show-offy, actually, but my mom was obviously enjoying her movie, and I didn't want to ruin it. I grabbed a handful of popcorn and shoved it into my mouth.

"Yeah, romantic," I said not too convincingly while I continued to chew.

A buzzing sound came from the basement. "Oh, that's the wash cycle finishing," my mom said, hopping up. "Don't pause it. I'll be right back." She came up the basement stairs five minutes later with the first load of clean laundry, which she folded while watching the female lead sob into a cappuccino with her best friend. Then, as soon as she finished that, my mother noticed that the mirror above the mantel was streaky. "I can clean it and watch at the same time," she said, getting up for the Windex and paper towels. By the time the couple was getting to the bottom of the whole similar-sweaters/mistaken-identity thing via a shouting match in Central Park followed by (surprise) a romantic kiss that cut to (surprise) their wedding day, my mother had moved on to dusting. So much for getting her to take a break. I sighed and picked up a dust rag as the credits rolled. If I couldn't beat her, my only option was to join her. We cleaned until ten that night and both fell into bed exhausted.

In a way, it was almost a relief to go back to school the next morning. At least in class I could sit down and have a quiet moment to myself.

But the quiet didn't last long. Dina started shrieking the second I saw her in the hallway between math and chemistry. "Look!" she said, pulling a scrap of paper out of her pocket. "I got it. On Saturday. You're making that cheesecake now. No excuses. *And* the pinwheel cookies. You can pay me out of your next check for the twenty-five-dollar donation to Panda Rescue, if you want. Or even the one after that. I was so nervous I thought I was going to pass out. I wanted to tell you, but you guys left together for your driving lesson. So I decided to wait until I saw you in person today, but it's been killing me." I took the piece of paper she was waving excitedly and examined the phone number written across it in crisp black ink. "I gave him my number, too. He said he'd call me tonight if he didn't get a chance to see me at the store first."

"Really?" I handed back the paper, a strange, heavy feeling filling my chest.

"Yeah. We're going to talk more about the party."

"Dina, that's great!" I said, biting my lip. I gave my head a shake. Seriously? What was wrong with me? Like I'd told Patrick, I didn't date; plus, even though he was a nice guy, Patrick got on my nerves every time he teased me (which was often); plus, I *wanted* him to like Dina. Everything was going completely according to plan for once. "That's really, really awesome."

It was so awesome, in fact, that I felt awesome about it all day long. I moped my way through chemistry and barely picked at my Caesar salad at lunch while Dina and her friends Carly and Cara planned decorations and came up with cheesy panda-themed party games. (Panda piñatas, pin the tail on the panda, and pass the panda present were just a few of the things I had to look forward to on Valentine's Day.)

And I felt about ten times more awesome when, halfway through our shift at the store, Dina's pocket started buzzing and, for once, it turned out *not* to be Damien. "Patrick!" Dina said, her eyes going wide—a huge smile breaking across her face. "How are you? Are you calling from the Keyhole?" She listened for a few seconds. "Oh no! Oooooh. Poor you," she cooed into the phone. "What's wrong? Un-huh." She twirled a lock of hair around one finger. "Oh my God. Un-huh." She switched the phone from one ear to the other. "Okay, I'll tell her. Feel better. I'll call you tomorrow, okay? Bye." She flipped her cell shut.

"That was Patrick," she said, like it wasn't blindingly obvious that I'd been hanging on every word of her end of the conversation. "Your driving lesson's canceled tonight. He's sick."

"Oh," I said. "Yay! No driving! Or, I mean, oh no. That sucks that he's sick. What's wrong?"

"He caught Lyme disease."

"You're kidding."

"No, that's what he said. It sounds really serious. Elyse, I'm worried about him."

"Yeah," I said. "Yeah, me too." Except that I was actually more confused than worried. I'd never heard of anyone in Middleford getting Lyme disease before, and I'd definitely, definitely never heard of anyone getting it in February. Wasn't it spread by deer ticks? There weren't any deer in town, and even if there were, wouldn't their ticks be busy nesting, watching deer tick TV, playing miniature games of deer tick poker, or doing whatever deer ticks did to pass the time until summer?

"If I pick out a card for him," Dina said, "and maybe some balloons, would you mind bringing them over to his house for me? I'd owe you big."

"Of course I wouldn't mind," I said. "You know I'm always happy to help you flirt."

I couldn't get over it. Dina had now let an entire two days pass without texting Damien back. It was a new record, and despite my weird reaction to the news that she and Patrick had exchanged numbers, I wasn't about to discourage her.

In retrospect, the only thing I wished is that I'd encouraged her to go with a nice "get well" decorative mug, or maybe a personalized smiley face key chain to cheer him up. Anything but the huge bunch of green helium balloons she put together, which I spent the next half hour trying not to bonk strangers on the head with as I rode the bus home. In fact, by the time I got to our street, I couldn't wait to get rid of the stupid things. I was planning to go straight over to Patrick's place to give them to him and to find out how he'd mysteriously contracted Lyme disease in February, but my mom was just pulling into the driveway. She got out of the car and started waving her arms frantically.

"Elyse!" she called. "Come into the house. Bring your balloons. We have to celebrate. You won't believe what happened to me at work today."

Chapter 7

My mom made me take off my coat and come into the kitchen before she'd tell me anything.

"You should sit," she said, pulling out a chair. My mind was racing, trying to figure out what could have happened at work to make her so excited. Did she get a massive raise? Did spa management already order her the new, ergonomically correct chair she'd asked for? Did Meg Ryan walk in off the street and give my mom her autograph before making a bikini wax appointment?

"No, no wait. You should stand up," my mom said. "No. Wait. It doesn't matter. I'll just tell you." She practically squealed. "We're going to Mexico!"

"What?" I asked.

"Cancun, Mexico." She pulled a brochure out of her purse and slapped it down on the table. I immediately recognized the bikini-clad couple on the front, sipping their neon-pink drinks. They were the same ones who'd taunted me while I shivered in the bus shelter outside the mall. "The resort is called Hotel Del Mar. It's a five-star facility. Ten days, nine nights, all expenses paid. They call it the 'Sweetheart Retreat,' but you don't need to be a couple to go. Sun, sand, and surf. We leave the day after tomorrow."

"What?" I said again. The news she was trying to tell me didn't make sense in so many ways. Mexico? The day after tomorrow? Five star? Us? As in me and my mother, whose last vacation—I don't know how many years ago—had included driving three hours down the highway to this dodgy-looking theme park called StoryBookLand, and staying at a motel that reeked of cigarettes and had no air-conditioning?

"I won the grand prize trip!" she exclaimed. "In the staff appreciation day raffle!"

"What?" I repeated. It was as if all other words had left me.

"I know!" she said. "I never win anything." Neither of us did. It was like a family curse. Half the time when I was a kid I didn't even get the prize the cereal box promised.

"I didn't even buy a ticket, and I *still* won."

"What?" I said, then caught myself, adding, "I mean, how is that possible?"

"It was Valter."

"Valter? Valter Big-ass-kiss?" I asked. My mother shot me a disapproving look, but then gave in and smiled. I mean, she'd just won a ten-day trip to Mexico. Who wouldn't be in a better-than-usual mood?

"He was in line behind me at the coat check, and he

asked if I'd bought my raffle tickets yet. I told him I didn't think I'd bother. But he said everyone deserved a chance at the grand prize, so he bought a ticket and put my name on it. Can you believe it? People spent hundreds of dollars in tickets, and I just had the one. I told Valter he must be a lucky charm."

Well, at least he had that much going for him. You'd need all the luck you could get in life with a name like that. I knew enough not to say any of that out loud, though.

"Mom, that's incredible," I said instead.

"I know," my mom went on. "Valter's just the nicest man. I tried to get him to take the vacation, since he'd paid for the ticket, but he flat-out refused. He said I should take my beautiful daughter."

"You have a beautiful daughter?" I said, looking over my shoulder, as if she might be standing behind me.

My mom didn't laugh. Self-deprecating humor was on her list of stuff she didn't find funny, right after making fun of people's names, apparently. "I have *the most* beautiful daughter," she answered seriously, then went straight back into her flustered mode. "The most beautiful daughter who needs a new bathing suit. And do your sandals from last summer still fit? Oh my God, we'll have to make sure your passport is up-to-date, too. You'll have to call Mr. Goodman and ask for the time off. And I'll let your school know. We'll have to reschedule your driving test, too, I suppose. I hope Patrick won't mind if you take a break from lessons for a while." She handed me the cordless phone along with the envelope my last paycheck had come in. She pointed to the store number. "Why don't you start with Mr. Goodman?"

And that was when our luck—or mine, at least—took a turn for the worse. Honestly, I should have been expecting it all along. Ten-day trips to Mexico didn't just fall from the sky into my life. "Elyse, you know I'd love to give you the time off," Mr. Goodman said after I'd explained the situation, "but with Valentine's Day coming up, I can't be training new staff right now. As it is, I barely have enough people to cover the shifts." At the same time, my mother walked back into the kitchen examining my passport—a devastated look on her face. Even from across the room, I could tell from a glimpse at the photo that I was about five years old in it, which meant it was way, way expired. I wasn't sure how long it took to apply for a new one, but I had a feeling it was more than a day.

"That's okay, Mr. Goodman," I said. "I completely understand." Sure, my heart was sinking a little—but just a little. I liked beaches and sun as much as anyone, and it would be great to get away—especially if it meant avoiding the whole Valentine's Day thing at home—but maybe it was for the best. I always got sunburns. I had a chemistry test on Friday that I'd already started studying for, and a social studies project due the following Tuesday. And, even though I was dreading it, it was better to get my driving test out of the way than to spend more time obsessing over it. Plus, Dina might never forgive me if she didn't get her cheesecake. . . .

"Maybe they'll make an exception about your passport at customs," my mom tried, "if we explain that I won the trip on short notice? And you could always quit at Goodman's and find a new job when we get back."

I sat down across from her. "Mom," I said reasonably. "I don't think so. If I quit Goodman's, it could take ages for me to find something else. Nobody at the mall is hiring right now. And isn't customs usually pretty strict about things like passports?"

"Well, then." She took a deep breath and reached for the phone. "I'll call Valter and tell him that's that. We can't go. He'll have to take the tickets instead."

"No, Mom. Wait." I slapped a hand on top of hers to stop her from dialing. "I'm seventeen. I can look after myself. *You* go." She gave me a doubtful look. "Take Carolynn." My mom and her best friend had been plotting for ages about how, when their kids were all grown up, they'd take a girls' trip to some Caribbean island. Now was obviously the time. "Or Aunt Sarah. I'll be fine here. I swear."

"I don't think so, Elyse. Carolynn probably can't get time off work on such short notice, and Sarah's got Uncle Tom's CD release on Wednesday night."

"So go with someone else. . . ."

"Who else would I go with?"

"I don't know. Anyone . . . It doesn't matter. Just go."

"If I left you here on your own, how would you get groceries?"

"Mom, I know where the store is. . . ."

"What if something breaks in the house?"

"I can use the phone as well as you can to call a repair person. . . ."

"You might be lonely."

"I'll live."

"I'd miss you."

"I'd miss you, too. But, Mom, when are you ever going to have a chance like this again? And when's the last time you had a real vacation? Plus, after how hard the last few months have been . . . this would be good for you. Seriously, it's about time you did something for yourself."

She shook her head like it was all too much to consider, and pulled her hand away, taking the phone with it. She reached for the white pages on the kitchen bookshelf, flipped through, and dialed a number. "Hello. Is this Valter?" she said into the receiver. I sighed heavily. "It's Michelle Ulrich. From work. Good, good. And you?" She paused. "Listen, I'm having a bit of a problem with those travel tickets from the raffle. My beautiful daughter can't get the time off work." She smiled at me across the table. "It's unfortunate, I know."

I stood up, pushing my chair back from the table noisily. Why did my mother have to be so stubborn about this? I was perfectly capable of taking care of myself. She should know that by now. When had I ever acted less than responsibly? Why did she have to go and ruin this one good thing that had happened in her life lately, just because of me? I opened the fridge and took out a yogurt cup, pulling the lid off angrily.

"So, anyway, I was wondering," my mom went on. "This might sound like a strange invitation—but there are two tickets. What if you and I went together?" I paused, spoon midway to my mouth. Had I just heard that right? "It only seems fair that you come along, since you paid for the raffle ticket in the first place. I'd be happy to pay for the extra hotel room, of course. . . . Really?" my mom said, her face breaking into a grin. "Okay. Well, that sounds perfect. Call me right back when you know for sure. Here. Let me give you my number." By the time my mom had hung up the phone, my mouth was hanging completely open.

"You know what, Elyse?" my mom said. "I think maybe you're right. Maybe it *is* about time I did something for myself."

Valter Bigaskis called back within the hour to say all the details were confirmed. He had rescheduled his clients' Swedish massage appointments. His favorite cat-sitter was available. The stars had aligned. "Great," I said, copying down the message. My mother had already dashed out to hit the mall before closing time. The elastic on her bathing suit, which she couldn't remember when she'd last worn, was all stretched out, and she'd need a new beach towel, and sunscreen, and a better suitcase, just to name a few things. "I'll let her know."

"Your modder," Valter said with a heavy accent, "iz like an angel. Did you know this?"

"Umm," I said. I wasn't used to strange Swedish men talking about my mother. I wasn't sure if I liked it. "Yeah, I guess. . . ."

"She's at the spa not even a veek, and already she looks out for everyone. Takes them under her ving. If dey need a coffee, she iz pouring it. If dey need to talk, she iz listening. A more deserving person could not vin dis vacation. I am honored to go vid her on a sveetheart retreat."

"Okay," I said, just wanting to get off the phone with this guy. "I'll be sure to tell her that. Bye-bye now."

"Yes," Valter went on. "Bye-bye now. And I look forward to meeting you soon, Meechelle's beautiful daughter."

"All right then," I said awkwardly. "Bye."

My initial relief and excitement that my mom was going on vacation to Mexico had suddenly turned into a weird apprehension. Did I really want my "angel" mother going on a "Sveetheart Retreat" with Valter the Swedish masseuse? What if they had a great time and became lifelong friends and he started coming over for Christmas dinner every year? Or, worse, what if they fell in love? And got married? And I had to change my last name to Bigaskis?

I grabbed Dina's bunch of green balloons and put on my coat, planning to head next door to Patrick's house. Maybe if I was lucky I could catch Lyme disease before Wednesday and my mom would decide to stay home after all.

Except that, the second I saw Patrick, I knew my plan

was destined to fail. Because unless people suffering from Lyme disease looked totally fine and one of the symptoms was a strange desire to dance around the kitchen waving utensils, Patrick was totally faking it. He was a pretty decent dancer, though, I had to admit. I knocked on the small window in the back door, catching him singing into a spatula and scaring him half to death. I could see the blush on his cheeks even though he was halfway across the room, but I didn't feel that bad. After all, he'd seen me doing the scuba in my living room window when I hadn't known he was watching, and that was just as embarrassing.

"Happy Lyme disease," I said, shoving the huge bunch of balloons through the door as soon as he opened it. "You look terrible." He blushed even more.

"Okay," he said, hanging his head a little as he turned off the music, which I had recognized instantly. It was "Gloria," by Van Morrison. It always made me dance around like a moron, too. "So I'm busted."

"*Very* busted."

I took in the disastrous scene in the old-fashioned kitchen. Half of the wood-paneled cupboard doors were wide open; mixing bowls, pots, and pans were spilling out onto the floor; the double sink was piled full of dishes; and there was flour all over everything: the brown-and-white flecked countertop, the cracked linoleum floor, Patrick's socks. Also, something was burning in a serious way. "You might want to deal with that." I pointed toward the huge, antique oven. Smoke was starting to come out of the vent underneath the back burner.

"Oh man." Patrick opened the oven door and reached for the cookie sheet inside.

"Wait," I called, but it was too late. He'd already touched it. With his bare hands.

"Ouch!" he yelped, hopping around. "Ow ow ow ow ow."

"Here." I turned on the cold water in the sink, grabbed his arm, and shoved his hand underneath. Then I reached for the oven mitts and pulled the tray out, shutting the heat off with my free hand at the same time. The tray was coated with a lumpy black mass of something that kind of looked like asphalt.

"They're cookies," Patrick said. "Oatmeal raisin. Or, they were." I walked over and checked his hand. Two of his fingertips were a bit red, but there were no blisters.

"I think you'll be okay," I said. "But you might want to put some Polysporin on later if it gets red." I let go of his hand, then walked over to poke at the edge of the "cookies" with Patrick's spatula. The batter had all run together into one mega-cookie, which was now cemented onto the baking sheet. "They look delicious," I quipped.

"Hey," he shot back. "I'm a beginner here. A little encouragement?" I suddenly regretted teasing him, especially in light of how patient he'd been with me in the car the day before. "You should see me in shop class. I can build a birdhouse in my sleep. I sanded my canoe paddle so well the teacher couldn't even find the seams in the wood . . . but this . . ." He took the spatula from me and poked at the blackened cookies. "This is nothing like woodworking."

"Well," I said, searching my brain for something positive to say. "You definitely cooked them very thoroughly."

Patrick laughed, and went to drop the spatula in the sink. "I'm glad you think so," he said. "They're for you." I stared at him. "To make up for the whole blossoming-Japanese-cherry-bush thing yesterday. I felt bad, okay? This was supposed to be my peace offering."

I was more than a little surprised. "You pretended to have Lyme disease so you could stay home and bake me cookies?"

"Not exactly. My buddy Jax from the Keyhole needed to pick up some extra shifts at work to cover a few bills. I called in sick so he could take the hours. Plus, I figured you wouldn't really want to go driving with me today . . . after the parking, and the bush. The Lyme disease thing was kind of off the top of my head." He pointed at a bag of limes that was sitting on the windowsill. "I've never been a very good liar." He motioned to a kitchen chair. "Have a seat. I'll get you some juice or something."

"No. Thanks, but really, I can't stay. My mom just won this crazy ten-day trip to Mexico, so I should help her get ready. She leaves Wednesday. I just came to bring you these balloons. And this card." I handed it over. "They're from Dina," I explained.

"And you." He'd already torn the envelope open.

"Huh?"

He showed me a signature that read "Elyse" in big, loopy writing, nothing like my own. "Oh, right," I said, not wanting to make Dina look bad, even though I was fully intending to kill her the next day. If she'd been planning to fake my signature, the least she could have done would have been to warn me. "I forgot. It's from me, too."

He flipped the card closed again. The cover had a picture of a bunny rabbit dressed in a lab coat. "Dr. Bunny thinks it just ain't funny when your nose is runny," he read, then opened the card. "Hope you're hopping down the road to recovery soon." I shoved my hands deep into my coat pockets, wishing I could vanish from the kitchen and never be associated with the embarrassing bunny card again. She couldn't have picked something with a nice neutral landscape on it?

"A joke card," he observed, like he was considering what that might mean. "But, it actually rhymes. Thanks." I looked up, expecting him to be mocking me, but his smile seemed sincere.

"Yeah, well. Dina picked it out," I explained quickly. "She was really worried about you. The balloons were her idea, too." I bopped one at his head. He bopped it back. Quick reflexes. It probably explained why he was such a good driver. "You know, lime green, for Lyme disease."

"That was really sweet of her," Patrick said, giving me an odd look.

"She's a sweet girl," I said. An awkward silence hung between us for a few seconds until it was thankfully interrupted by the sound of the oven timer going off. "Anyway," I continued. "Like I said, I'd better get going. Thanks for the attempted cookies. You really didn't need to do that, you know. I wasn't *that* mad."

"Yes, you were," he said. "And, yes, I did. I have to prove to you that I'm in the other two percent." It took me a second to figure out what he was talking about. "You know, not a pig. Except, I guess it didn't quite work out." He picked up a butter knife and tried to pry the corner of the blackened cookie lump off the pan. "Plus, now I have the whole lying-to-you-about-having-Lyme-disease thing to feel bad about, too. I can't believe you brought me balloons."

"Mostly from Dina," I reminded him quickly. But I'm not sure if he heard me. He was already reaching for his cookbook.

"I can't figure out what went wrong. Maybe I used too much melted butter. It said three quarters of a cup, but they looked dry, so I put extra. Then they looked wet, so I put more raisins. Or maybe it's because I didn't sift the flour. How do you sift flour, anyway?"

"It was probably the butter," I said, opening the back door a crack.

"Yeah. Probably," he said thoughtfully. He tossed the cookbook onto the kitchen table. "You know, I was wrong. Baking isn't like parallel parking at all. It's way harder."

* * *

My mom got home from the mall about an hour later, a new bathing suit in hand. It was covered in bright orange and pink flowers and had a shockingly low neckline, but she looked so excited about it that I tried not to raise my eyebrows.

"It's a little daring, isn't it?" she said, an unfamiliar glow in her cheeks that I was pretty sure had nothing to do with the temperature (–18 with windchill).

"You can always wear a wrap over it," I suggested. "And the colors are nice and bright. You'll blend in with the Mexican foliage."

After that, I went upstairs to get started on some homework and leave her to do her preparations and packing. It was almost nine, and I'd just finished studying for my chemistry test and stepped into the shower, when I heard the doorbell ring. My mom came up the stairs a few minutes later.

"Patrick next door dropped these off for you," she said, knocking on my bedroom door as I unwrapped the towel turban from my head. "He shovels the driveway *and* he bakes. I told you he was a nice boy. I thought you might want one before bed." She picked up a cookie and took a bite. "They're still warm. Really, Elyse. He's too sweet. Why don't you ask him to that party Dina's having? It could be fun."

I tried not to roll my eyes. "Because I'm not interested, Mom. And neither is he. That's why."

As soon as she left I changed into my pajamas, then

picked a cookie up off the plate. They were moist this time, and lightly browned. I bit in. Amazing, really, for a beginner. I ate a second, then a third. And that's when I discovered it, resting against the very bottom of the plate—an oatmeal cookie shaped like a heart. A perfect heart. Obviously not accidental. I picked it up, turning it over in my hands as a queasy feeling filled my stomach.

Suddenly, things fell into place. Patrick's strange obsession with ballpoint pens, his question about which valentine to buy, the way he'd asked in the driveway the day before about whether or not I was taking my boyfriend to the panda party. He wasn't interested in Dina. For some inexplicable reason, he had a crush on *me* and—worse—he'd just declared it, in cookie form.

I sank down on the bed, feeling overwhelmed by the mess I'd somehow gotten myself into. Then I ate the evidence before my mother could find it.

Chapter 8

By the time Wednesday morning came around, my mother had officially lost her mind. Aside from packing way too much stuff (seriously, how many pairs of flip-flops does a person traveling to Mexico for ten days need?), she had also attached sticky notes to almost every surface in the house. "Back burner heats slow," read one on the kitchen counter. "Call Parson Plumbing at 555-867-2525 if toilet backs up. Drano under sink if bathtub clogs," instructed another on the bathroom door. And that's saying nothing of the humongo list of emergency numbers and random instructions on the table. "If you need anything, call Carolynn or Aunt Sarah. Keep windows closed and locked *at all times*. Garbage goes out Monday P.M. *Do not let strangers into the house!!!*"

"Mom," I said, holding up the list. "You *do* realize I'm not twelve, right?"

"I know," she said, rewrapping the power cord for her blow-dryer and placing it in her carefully organized luggage. "I know, it's just, you've never been home alone this many days in a row. I can't help but worry."

"I'll be fine."

"I know you will. Oh," she exclaimed, whipping her sticky notes and pen out of her back pocket. "I can't believe I almost forgot." She started scribbling furiously. "Before you go to bed tonight, double-check all the locks, and test all the smoke alarms and the carbon monoxide detector. Promise me? And I should probably leave you the number for poison control, just in case you accidentally—"

"Mom," I interrupted her. "I'm not going to accidentally eat poisonous things. Trust me." She took a deep breath, then scrunched up the sticky note. "You're right. I'm being ridiculous." She came over and kissed the top of my head.

"I have to go now, okay? Or I'll be late for school. Have *fun,*" I said, emphasizing the word. "Try to forget that winter exists. And don't worry about me."

"I will. I mean, I won't," she said. "I mean, I'll try not to worry. I love you."

"I love you, too," I answered.

"Oh, and Elyse," my mom added as I stepped over the threshold. "I asked Patrick's grandfather if the two of them wouldn't mind checking in on you occasionally." I sighed. "Just in case there's anything you need help with . . . since they're right next door. I don't think you realize how much work it can be to look after everything on your own," she went on when she saw the withering look I was giving her. "It's good to have backup."

"Right," I said sarcastically. "In case there's a pickle jar I can't open and I need the handsome boy next door to rush to my rescue."

"Really?" my mom said, totally missing my point. Her eyes lit up. "Did I just hear you say you think Patrick next door is handsome?"

I groaned and turned to go. I was *not* about to have this discussion with my mother. "Good-bye," I said instead. "Have a margarita for me. Virgin, obviously," I added when she raised an eyebrow. "I'll see you on the fifteenth."

That afternoon, traffic was lighter than usual (maybe everyone had jumped on a plane to Mexico along with my mother), which meant that Dina and I were a full fifteen minutes early getting to the mall for work.

"Oh," Dina said, grabbing my arm. "Can we go into American Apparel for a sec? They have these new micro-mesh minidresses in black and white. I want to try one on. I might get it for the panda party."

"Seriously?" I said as she pulled me into the store. I'm not a prude or anything, but the white dress in size zero was being modeled by a particularly twiglike headless mannequin. The thing was practically see-through. "Why don't you just go naked? It'd be cheaper. . . ."

"You wear another shirt underneath it, silly. Plus, I'd get leggings. It's cute though, right?" She took one off the rack and held it against her to check the size. "Do you think Patrick would like it?"

I hesitated. All through lunch hour that day, I'd been trying to work up the nerve to tell Dina about Patrick's heart-shaped cookie confession. I'd even tried to broach the subject once by bringing up the fake Lyme disease and my forged signature on the card . . . both of which I'd hoped would take me up to the cookie part, but I never quite got there.

"Oh my God. I meant to tell you I signed your name," Dina had apologized instead. "I didn't think you'd mind. It's just . . ." She'd paused, biting her lip nervously. "I don't want to seem desperate when I'm flirting with him. Damien always said I was too clingy, you know?" I made a face like I thought that was the most outrageous thing I'd ever heard, but she didn't buy it. "I know I come on strong sometimes, and that I get attached too easily. I just think Patrick is someone I could totally see myself with. Long-term, you know, even five years from now. I *so* don't want to mess this up. Whatever you do, Elyse, you *can't* let him know I have a crush on him, okay? I want to take it really slow so I don't freak him out."

I'd gulped, then nodded. Five years from now? She'd barely known Patrick a week, and already she was practically planning to marry the guy. This was way more serious than your average crush. Plus, getting her to like him had been all my idea in the first place. If I broke her heart now—and with Valentine's Day right around the corner—she'd go back to semi-stalking Damien, and I'd officially be the crappiest friend in the whole world.

I'd eaten my cafeteria Jell-O and silently revised my plan. The best way to deal with this would be to talk to Patrick, and to be honest. Well, partly honest, anyway. I'd tell him flat-out that I wasn't interested in him that way—that I just wanted to be neighbors; and driving instructor and student; and friends, and then I'd hope like hell that I could convince him how wonderful Dina was without actually revealing to him that she had a superbad crush on him. Simple, right? Totally.

"If I try the black, will you try the white?" Dina asked, holding a micro-mesh mini out to me, a hopeful look on her face. "Here." She grabbed some camisoles and leggings off another rack before I could say no. "Please. I'm too chicken to try it on alone."

Five minutes later, against my better judgment, I was wriggling out of my jeans in a cramped changing room while I listened to Dina chatter excitedly about party plans on the other side of the wall. "Mr. Goodman is donating black and white helium balloons *and* panda-themed paper plates. I know they're not the most environmentally responsible choice, but they're just so cute. And I figure we can limit it to one plate per person to minimize waste."

"Dina," I said anxiously. "I think we have a problem."

"You're right," she sighed. "It's still wasteful. I should probably tell him thanks, but no, right?"

"No. It's not about the paper plates." I stared at myself in the full-length mirror. The leggings Dina had picked out for me had to be a size double-zero—if such a thing existed. They were so short that they barely covered my knees, and so tight that my stomach bulged over the top. The camisole was even tinier. I was a reasonably thin, flattish-chested person, but even I couldn't pull it down over my boobs properly. "The camisole is way too small. The pants are tiny, too."

"Okay. Just gimme a sec to finish changing. I'll go get you different ones." I waited, shivering slightly. "What about the dress? Does it fit? Try it on over your bra, okay? That way I can get you another micromini, too, if it's the wrong size." I pulled the dress over my head. It fit, but that didn't mean it looked good. For one thing, I was still wearing the tummy-bulge leggings, but that wasn't the worst of my problems.

That morning, the laundry situation had been verging on desperate, and I'd ended up wearing my grossest-ever underwear—a super comfortable, but extra-embarrassing Christmas-themed bra and panties set covered in candy canes and little reindeer. My mom had given it to me the year before, and I'd worn it so often there were holes where the underwire had rubbed through the bra. I'd also accidentally put it in the wash a time or two or three with red towels, so the fabric was a sickish pink color. All that, plus the tiny red noses of the Rudolphs were shining brightly through the sheer white micro mesh, making it look like I had some strange boob rash.

"Do you have it on? Does it fit?" Dina asked again.

"Yeah. The dress part fits," I said miserably.

"Just a sec, 'kay? I'll grab you a new camisole and leggings." While she was gone, I tried not to make direct eye contact with myself in the mirror. It was too horrifying. "That's the only size of white camisole they've got," Dina said from outside the changing room door a minute later. "And for leggings, they've got that, or extra large."

"Oh darn," I said happily. "Guess I'll have to pass on the dress then."

"No, wait," Dina urged. "I want to see what it looks like on you, at least. And you have to see the black on me so I can get your honest opinion."

"No way. Nuh-uh. Not coming out. Not ever," I said. "Not until I change into my regular clothes. Sorry."

"Please? Just open the door a crack. I swear, there's nobody out here."

"Okay, fine," I sighed. "I'm opening the door for one second, and one second only. You aren't allowed to laugh, and then I'm closing it again. Ready?" I pushed the changing room door open about half an inch, then half an inch more. "Oh my God, Dina," I exclaimed, peeking through the crack. She was standing out in the open near the full-length mirror, twirling around. "That looks incredible on you."

Her soft curves pushed the sheer black fabric out in all the right places, and the camisole and leggings made the look sexy, but not indecent.

"Do you think?"

"Definitely." If Patrick saw her in that, convincing him to have a crush on her instead of on me would be a cinch.

"I think the zipper might be broken, though," she said, reaching over her shoulder with one hand and fiddling with it. "It gets stuck at the top."

"Let me see." And that was my fatal mistake. Without even thinking, I stepped out of the changing room and walked toward her, reindeer bra on full display for the world to see.

"Come and tell me if these are too tight," I heard someone say from the other end of the hallway. A girl was opening her changing room door. I should have recognized her voice, but I didn't. Not right away. *His* voice, though, sent shivers down my spine instantly.

"Nah. Nothing's too tight on you, according to me."

I turned. Why? I don't know. Probably out of shock, or stupidity. Or both.

"Elyse?" Matt Love, my ex-boyfriend, was staring directly at me. No, correction: Matt Love, my ex-boyfriend, was staring directly at my Rudolphs. I froze, blinking at him like a reindeer in the headlights. Then I came to my senses and crossed my arms awkwardly over my chest.

I hadn't seen Matt in nearly eight months, since last June, when tenth grade finished for the summer. After that, I'd begged my mom to let me enroll early at Sir Walter Scott High in the neighborhood we were planning to move to. But even though it had been a long time, besides the fact that his hair was a bit longer at the sides and he was wearing a T-shirt I didn't recognize, he didn't look all that different. Matt Love smiled at me—that same slow, slightly crooked smile I remembered—and my heart started hammering with a mixture of panic and fury, the same way it used to when I'd pass him in the halls at my old school after that fateful February 14. "How's it going?"

Before I had time to answer, my former best friend Tabby stepped out of her changing room in a pair of white, skin-tight jeans. All of her attention was focused on Matt Love as she pranced in front of him, shaking her butt. "What do you think?" She took both his hands in hers and wrapped his arms around her waist from behind, pressing her body against his and leaning back. She tipped her head to look into his eyes, and that was when she noticed the distracted look on his face. She followed his gaze. "Elyse?!" she exclaimed, hugging Matt's arms even more tightly around her. Her voice had a fake-friendly tone that made my stomach lurch. "What are you doing here?"

"I work here," I said numbly.

"At American Apparel? Seriously?"

I didn't answer. Just because I'd moved to another school, and just because nearly a year had passed, it didn't change the way I felt about her. I had nothing to say.

"Hey, do you get discounts?" she asked.

Tabby, while once fun to hang out with, had never been the brightest person on earth. Did she honestly think I'd be wearing a see-through dress over supertight leggings and a reindeer bra if I was working a shift there? And even if I did work there, did she truly believe I'd be buying her skanky jeans with my employee discount after she stole my boyfriend and stabbed me in the back?

"Yeah," I said, looking at her squarely. "I get an awesome employee discount. Forty percent." Then I turned, marched into the changing room, and slammed the door so hard the mirrors shook. I hugged my arms around myself and pressed my back into the corner, closing my eyes tightly against the tears that were threatening to start flowing.

Outside in the hallway, I could hear Tabby and Matt talking.

"God! Hold a grudge much?" Tabby was saying. "If I had a forty percent employee discount, I'd totally offer to buy her stuff. I mean, we used to be friends. I used to do everything for her."

"Let it go." Matt tried to soothe her. "She really liked me, okay? She's just still pissed about what happened."

"That was ages ago. It's been, like, almost an entire year." They were close enough that I could hear the sound of Tabby's gum squishing between her teeth. "But I guess some people never get over stuff." She sighed, then seemed to brighten. "Oh my God, though. That just made me realize. Can you even believe it, Matty? We've been together almost an entire year. I'm getting these. They look hot, right? I'm totally going to wear them on our anniversary." I bit hard on my bottom lip to keep a sob from escaping. A few seconds later, I heard the sound of her changing room door closing.

"Elyse?" Dina whispered from the hallway. I didn't

answer. I couldn't risk opening my mouth. I was determined that Matt Love was *not* going to hear my voice crack. Tabby was *not* going to know she'd made me cry. Another door closed. "Elyse?" I heard the whisper again, this time near my feet. I jumped. There was Dina's face, sticking through the gap underneath the partition between our two changing rooms. "Are you okay?"

The tears started running down my cheeks. I couldn't stop them. "Elyse," she whispered again. "I'm coming over." If I hadn't been so totally destroyed, I might even have laughed. Instead of standing up and coming through the door, like a normal person might have, Dina pushed her head all the way through the gap, then wriggled her shoulders frantically until they somehow slid through. The rest of her body followed more easily, but it still wasn't pretty—especially considering how small both changing rooms were, and the fact that she was wearing a see-through minidress.

Finally, she pushed herself to her feet and put her arms around me. She didn't ask a single question while I cried, soaking the barely existent fabric covering her shoulder.

We stood there, huddled in the corner, until we heard the changing room door opening and closing again, and Matt's and Tabby's voices receding down the hallway toward the cash.

Dina stepped back and brushed a strand of tear-soaked hair off my cheek.

"Sorry. Those people were—" I started to explain, but

the words got choked off by my sobs.

"Matt Love, right? And Tabby? Your ex and your former best friend." I nodded. "Yeah. I figured. Assholes," she muttered under her breath.

Hearing sweet, sensitive Dina use a swear word caught me so off guard that I actually stopped crying for a second.

"What?" she said, looking at me indignantly. "They are! I'm sorry, but you don't treat a friend that way. And you definitely, definitely don't do that to someone you claim to love. Come on," she said, moving another chunk of tear-soaked hair off my face. "Get changed. I'll go out first to make sure the coast is clear." I nodded and she lay down on the floor, starting to rewriggle into her own changing room, feet first.

"Dina?" I said. She stopped and looked up. There were so many things I wanted to say to her right then. "Thank you" was near the top of the list. And "I promise I'll never do something like that to you" was a close second. But she looked so worried, and going all schmoopy on her wasn't going to help matters—which probably explains why my first instinct was to make a joke. Something to let her know I was going to be all right. "Please don't make me buy this dress, okay?" She smiled, clearly relieved.

"Yeah," she admitted, looking up from the floor. "That's maybe not the best look for you."

"You think?" I said, sniffing. I stuck out my reindeer

boobs and looked in the mirror. "It's festive."

She laughed. Then her head disappeared underneath the partition again. I looked in the mirror and wiped at my cheeks with the back of my hand. Strangely enough, I was feeling better now. A lot better. I mean, yeah, I was still sad about what had happened with Matt Love last year. I still had no intention of opening up my heart to that kind of hurt again, but when it came to Tabby, I suddenly didn't care anymore. So what if we weren't friends? She'd been kind of crazy and fun to hang out with—always up on the latest gossip about who liked who and which teachers secretly smoked behind the football field—but the truth was, she was mean. She'd *always* been mean. In a lot of ways, she'd never really been much of a friend to begin with.

"I'm not getting this dress either," Dina said from the other side of the wall. "It looks awful."

"No, it doesn't," I said. "It makes *me* look like a sausage link. But on you, it looks amazing. You should get it."

"It *so doesn't* make you look like a sausage link," she said, but she hesitated a second too long before saying it. "Okay. So it *does* look a little bit terrible on you," she admitted, "but it's still better than Miss Thing's tight jeans. Did you see her butt in those?" Dina whispered. "It was so flat you couldn't tell if she was walking backward or forward."

"Dina!" I whispered back. My jaw dropped.

"I'm serious though." She changed the subject. "I'm

not getting this dress." I heard her changing room door open. "It's got bad associations now. If I wear this to the party, all you're going to think about is Matt Love and Pancake Butt. I'll find something else." I heard the clink of the metal hanger against the rejects rack as she hung it up.

"Dina, honestly," I started, "you should get it." But she didn't hear me. She'd already gone out into the store to make sure Matt and Tabby had left.

Dina Marino, I thought—as I yanked my jeans up and put the horrific transparent dress back on its hanger—sweet, loyal, loving, passionate about the things she believed in, and surprisingly catty when the moment called for it. Now *that* was a true friend.

Chapter 9

Because of the whole terrible Matt Love/see-through dress episode, we ended up being almost ten minutes late for our shift. Mr. Goodman was pacing the floor in the day-planner section when we got there, obviously annoyed about the fact that his dinner was at home getting cold.

"Girls," he said. "If you need help remembering what time your shift begins, might I remind you that we carry a wide selection of planners and agendas."

"I'm really sorry, Mr. Goodman," I said, taking my name tag out of my backpack and pinning it on.

"It was my fault," Dina cut in. I shot her a look. "My, um, watch battery died." I glanced at her wrist. She wasn't wearing a watch. Thankfully Mr. Goodman either didn't notice or didn't care.

"Do your best to keep it from happening again," he said. "That's all I ask. In any case"—he walked to the cash and we followed—"you can make it up to me. Sales are still slow." He patted Cupid's head. "So I'm starting a new incentive program for staff. For every ten new customers you sign up for the customer loyalty card between now and Valentine's Day, I'll add fifty dollars to your paychecks." Our eyes went wide. Fifty dollars was *a lot* of money, considering we only made minimum wage.

By the time Mr. Goodman left two minutes later, Dina had already done the do-gooder math in her head. "You realize if we sign up a hundred people, and add that money to what we collect at the party, we'll be able to sponsor two pandas. A hundred people is nothing. That's just twelve or thirteen people per shift. We can totally do that!" My head was still achy from crying in the dressing room. My heart still felt heavy. I had a hard time sharing her enthusiasm and—honestly—if I had an extra fifty bucks, I wanted to spend it on a really good blond wig. That way, I could disguise myself at work and never risk Matt or Tabby spotting me at the mall again. . . . But Dina looked so optimistic. And after she'd been there for me at American Apparel, I didn't want to let her down.

"We'll have to be aggressive though," she went on. "We can't just sit back."

I nodded vaguely, then slit open the packing tape on a box of merchandise Mr. Goodman had left us to shelve. Inside were mini boxes of heart-shaped chocolates with love propaganda written on them in pink bubble letters: *You complete me. Be mine always. I adore you.* Seriously, I didn't know if I could take nine more days of this. It was beyond cruel when even my favorite food reminded me how broken my heart was.

I tried to count off the boxes against the packing slip, but I was also eyeing the entryway to make sure Matt Love and Tabby weren't about to walk in, staring smushily into each other's eyes. I kept getting my numbers screwed up.

"This can't be right," I said, crossing out my total for the third time. "The packing slip says thirty boxes, but there must be, like, one-thirty here."

"Let me see," Dina said, coming around the cash. She started counting. "You're right. One-thirty exactly. They overshipped."

I sighed as I separated out thirty chocolates and started to pile the others back into the box. "Mr. Goodman will have to return the rest, I guess."

"No. Wait," Dina said. "I just had an idea." She had a strange glint in her eye. "The slip says thirty, right? It's not like the supplier is going to remember where the extras went. And, besides." She picked up the packing slip. "They were shipped from British Columbia. If we sent them back now, they'd never get back to the warehouse in time for Valentine's Day. And they'll have gone bad by next year. They'd basically be wasted."

"Dina?" I raised my eyebrows. "If you're thinking what I think you're thinking . . ."

"It's for a good cause," she added, ignoring my warning tone. She grabbed the sample Cupid doll in one hand and the box of chocolates in the other. "Cupid and I will be out in the mall corridor," she said, pressing his tummy to start him up. "I'll send them in, you sign them up."

I had to hand it to her. Legally speaking, what she was doing might have qualified as stealing—just a little bit—but it also worked. Because, as it turns out, free chocolate will make people do just about anything. By four o'clock that day, I'd signed up forty people for the customer loyalty plan. At four fifteen, number forty-one walked in, grinning at me. He took off his giant DJ earphones and set his box of free chocolates down on the counter.

"These are for you," he said, sliding the box toward me. *You're so huggable.* I left them sitting awkwardly on the counter between us. "I want to sign up, but I just have one question. Do pens count toward this customer loyalty thing, or just cards?"

Not that I had any reason to notice, but he looked great. Patrick was wearing a crisp button-down shirt and jeans that fell off his hips just a little. He seemed relaxed, and even more cheerful than usual—obviously his two-day bout of fake Lyme disease had given him lots of time to rest.

"Just cards," I answered. "Sorry."

"Too bad," Patrick said, filling out the sign-up form I passed him, "because I need a new one. That pen you sold me last time—it really does make a crisp line, but now that I've had some time to think about it, it's almost too crisp, you know?"

"Too crisp," I repeated, trying to strike a professional tone. There was a playful look in his eyes I didn't like. Now that the cookie had revealed all, I could plainly see that he was flirting with me and, considering that Dina was just outside, it made me more than a little nervous.

"Do you have anything that writes really smooth? You know those pens where the ink just kind of rolls out?"

"Rolly," I said with a straight face. "Not sploodgy or crisp. I think we have just the thing." He followed me to the pen section where we fell into our already familiar routine. I'd hand him a pen, he'd test it on the scraps of paper and make thoughtful faces, then I'd hand him another option.

"So?" he said kind of casually after a while. "How did I do?"

"Do?"

"You know, with the cookies?"

I gulped. This was the part of the day I'd been dreading—the moment where I'd have to tell him that, as delicious as the cookies had been, his crush was unrequited.

"Yeah. About that . . ." I started. "The cookies—the second attempt—weren't bad. They were really good, actually. You obviously followed the recipe, b—" But my "but" got cut off by Dina's excited voice coming down the aisle.

"Elyse!" she squealed. "I just counted the forms. I can't believe it! Forty-one customer loyalty cards. That's over two hundred dollars. We're practically halfway there, and it's only the first day."

"Dina, that's awesome," I said, partly because it was true, and partly for Patrick's benefit. "It's all thanks to you, you know. You're so charming and friendly. Between you and the chocolate, who could resist?" She beamed. "Hey," I said, thinking on my feet. "You know what, Patrick? Dina here knows *everything* about pens. She can probably help you better than I can. Plus, I have that last box of merchandise to unpack before our driving lesson starts. So . . ." I trailed off, already walking away.

It didn't take Dina long to shift into full-flirtation mode. "I *love* your hair," I heard her say as I retreated down the aisle. "I wish I could get mine to go like that. Are those curls natural? For real? Okay, let me show you our best pens. If you promise not to tell anyone, I can even give you my employee discount."

I exhaled heavily as I stepped behind the cash where Cupid was, once again shaking his diapered butt. A bunch of eleven- or twelve-year-old girls were standing near the card display, watching and gossiping.

"That doll is sooooo cute," one of them said.

"I'm going to tell Nick G. that you want one for Valentine's Day," teased another, which made the first girl shriek and pretend-hit her friend.

"If you do, I'm killing you."

"He'd probably buy it for you, too. You know he has a crush on you. *Everyone* can tell. You're *so* lucky. Nobody *ever* has a crush on me," the second girl whined dejectedly.

"Hey," I said, joining their conversation, uninvited, from behind the cash. "Don't stress about it. You're probably just too smart. Guys get intimidated by that. Plus, there are worse things than nobody having a crush on you." Like the *wrong person* having a crush on you, I thought. But instead of listening to the wise advice of their elder, a few of them just rolled their eyes. Then they all walked away—one giant cluster of sixth-grade giggles. I tried not to take it personally. When I was their age, I wouldn't have believed me either.

Fifteen minutes later, as Patrick and I walked across the icy parking lot toward his red car, I mentally rehearsed what I was going to say: *"You're a great guy, don't get me wrong . . . but I'm just not interested in dating. . . . We should still be friends/neighbors/people who work at the same mall. . . . It's for the best. . . . You'll find someone else—someone who cares as much as you do about the plight of homeless people . . . someone who looks out for the welfare of helpless animals, perhaps . . . someone who loves your hair. . . ."*

Sure, it was probably going to make for an awkward driving lesson, but it was the kind of thing that was best done quickly—like ripping off a Band-Aid. He'd really only known me a week, anyway, and I hadn't always exactly been nice to him in that time. How serious about liking me could he actually be?

Apparently, the answer to that question was about to be

revealed to me in surprising detail.

"Wait, wait," Patrick said as we walked around the column for parking row C-10. "Close your eyes."

"Why?"

"Because I have a surprise for you."

"Is it a unicorn?" I said sarcastically.

"No," he answered.

"Okay. Then forget it. I'm not closing my eyes."

"It's better than a unicorn," he tried. Now, that, I found hard to believe. Not that I'd been into unicorns since I was six or seven years old—but still, a real, live unicorn in the SouthSide Mall parking lot would be pretty unbeatable when it came to surprises.

"Even if it *is* better than an enchanted magical horse with a golden horn—which is impossible," I countered, "it's not safe to walk through a parking lot with your eyes closed."

"I won't let anything happen to you. I'll hold your hand," he promised, which, considering the situation, didn't do much to make me feel better. The only reason I eventually gave in was because it was cold. I didn't want to stand out there arguing all day.

"Okay. Fine," I said, but I shoved both hands into my pockets, forcing him to hold my arm instead. I closed my eyes. "This'd better be good."

He steered me carefully over the icy patches and around parked cars. I heard him fumble with his keys. "Okay," he said as he opened the door. "You can look now." There, stuffed into the cup holders in the front seat, were a dozen red roses—or, to be more exact—a dozen, red, *dead* roses. Each rose's long stem was slumped over in a different direction—as if the weight of their big flowery heads had suddenly become too much to bear. On a scale of one to ten, with one being nothing at all and ten being the unicorn, they were definitely no higher than a two.

"Oh no," Patrick said, diving past me into the car when he saw. "They weren't like that this morning." He tried to prop the floppy stems up against the dash but they just wilted over again. "I swear. The lady I bought them from said they'd probably last three days. Maybe I wasn't supposed to leave them out in the cold," he said, scratching underneath the brim of his blue and white hat.

I stood, shifting my feet in the snow. "Flowers like water, too," I added unhelpfully. The exposed bottoms of the roses' stems were sticking through the cup holders and resting against the floor mat.

"Yeah. I've heard people say that." He sighed. "Okay, never mind. You must be freezing." He climbed out of the driver's seat to let me in. "There's another surprise, anyway." He ran around and got in. I shut the door, dreading whatever was coming next.

Patrick turned the key in the ignition and hit the power button on the CD player. Soft music filled the car. Even though I'd only heard them once—during our last driving lesson—I recognized the band as Surely Sarah. This was a slower song, though. A romantic song. Patrick turned to me.

"Elyse," he started. I could tell he was nervous. "Since the very first time I saw you through your window, I've thought you were beautiful . . . not to mention a kick-ass interpretive chair dancer. I mean, that scuba move, c'mon. . . ." He just *had* to tease me about that, didn't he? I gave him a look, but he just kept going, using a more serious tone now. "And, now that I'm getting to know you, I'm starting to really like you. You're so smart, and so funny. And, this song kind of says everything I've been wanting to say to you for a little while now, so—"

I couldn't let him go on. The smell of dead roses was overpoweringly sweet. The singer's voice was sickeningly sentimental. The look in Patrick's eyes was so intense it made me squirm. I reached over and hit the power button on the CD player. The car fell silent.

"Stop, Patrick," I said. "Please." He stared at me expectantly. "Look, I told you the other day. I don't date. So . . ." I picked up a rose, then let it flop again. "While this is all really nice, really sweet, honestly, I'm not interested in having a boyfriend. If that's what you were about to ask me." He looked heartbroken. "It's not you," I went on, "it's just, like I told you, I'm really focused on school right now. Plus, I've done the boyfriend thing before. It didn't end well."

"That's because you dated one of *them*," he said.

"One of who?"

"One of the ninety-eight percent. Look, when I was talking to Dina in the hallway today, she told me about what happened with your ex last year. She said you ran into the guy today at American Apparel. So, probably this"—he lifted a rose and let it flop, too—"wasn't the greatest timing." He squinted his eyes shut for a second. "When Dina told me what happened, I should have come out to the car and thrown the flowers out before you could see them. I could have bought more later. They were only twelve fifty."

"Honestly, Patrick," I said. "It wouldn't have mattered. I'm just . . . off the market right now."

"Right," he said, staring out the windshield. "Okay. I get that. You can't rush these things."

I had a feeling this was going to be a long, long driving lesson. "But hey," I went on as brightly as I could manage. "We're still friends, right?" I waited anxiously for him to answer. It was weird, but in the week or so that I'd known him, I'd already gotten used to having Patrick around. I liked his sweet, yet sometimes annoying ways; his cool, mellow music; his quirky sense of humor. I was even starting to think his strange obsession with finding the perfect pen was sort of charming. I didn't want to lose him altogether or have things be weird between us. "Plus, we've only got eight days left before my road test," I went on, "and I can't do a three-point turn to save my life. So what are we doing sitting around having awkward conversations?"

"Absolutely," he said. "Still friends." I breathed a sigh of relief. "And you're right. We should get going. We need to make you into . . ." He paused, thinking.

"The Tchaikovsky of three-point turns," I helped him out.

"Exactly." He turned the heat up. "And when we're done that, you can work on becoming the Hemingway of highway merging." I let my head fall back against the seat. He knew I hated highway driving more than anything—more than parallel parking, even. Clearly, he was punishing me for not wanting to be his girlfriend.

"So, are we driving, or are we sitting here all day smelling the dead roses?" he asked.

I checked my rearview mirror. "We're driving," I said, backing oh-so-carefully out of the space.

Chapter 10

Having (narrowly) survived my high-speed highway merging lesson—not to mention the weirdness with Patrick in the parking lot, and the horror of running into my ex while wearing a see-through dress and reindeer bra—I was relieved to turn the key in the lock and step into my very quiet house that night. My *very own, very quiet* house. I hung my coat up and walked into the kitchen, flipping on the light and feeling free. What should I do first? Eat chocolate for dinner? Turn the stereo up so loud the walls shook? Close all the curtains and dance around naked?

In the end, I settled for heating up one of the microwave dinners my mom had stocked the freezer with, sinking down onto the couch, and reading the book I was assigned for English class. Yeah. I'm wild and crazy like that. The phone rang a moment after I'd finished chapter three and scooped the last bite of pasty mashed potatoes out of the plastic tray.

"Elyse! We just arrived at the hotel here. How are you?" My mom's voice sounded crackly and far away. "Is everything all right with the house, sweetie?"

"Everything's great," I said, "except for this one wall that caved in." Even from halfway around the world and over a bad phone line, I could hear the unmistakable sound of my mother *not* laughing. "It's fine, Mom." I tried to reassure her. "No problems. I just got home from my driving lesson. I merged."

"That's wonderful, honey." I could hear music in the background now. And somebody laughing. "And how was work?"

"Great," I lied. There was no point telling her I'd seen Matt and Tabby. I wanted her to enjoy her vacation, not worry about me having an emotional breakdown. "Dina and I are selling lots of stupid Cupids."

"Oh. Just a second, Elyse." I could hear Valter's voice asking a question. "Yes! Why not? I'd love a margarita, thanks," my mom answered. "Did you remember to double-check that all the doors are locked?" she asked me, coming back on the line. "And the windows, too?"

"I'll do it before I go to bed," I said.

"Oh, good. And you're sure you're okay? Because, you know that if you need anything, you can call Auntie Sarah, or Carolynn, or ask the neighbors."

"I'm okay, Mom. Go. Drink your margarita. Don't worry about a thing."

"Okay, honey," she said. The music was getting louder now. Maracas were shaking. Someone whistled loudly. Where was she, anyway? Some kind of nightclub? If so, it had obviously been Valter's idea. My mom was usually in bed by ten. "I miss you," she added.

"I miss you, too," I said. "Good night." I hung up the phone and sat back down on the couch. It was so quiet in the house now that I could hear the faint rumbling of the furnace cycling on in the basement; the creak of the sofa springs when I shifted my weight; the windowpanes rattling ever-so-slightly in the wind. I grabbed the remote and turned on the TV, flipping through the channels, past the crime-scene investigation shows that were guaranteed to freak me out. The only relatively nonscary thing I could find was *American Super Model*. The girls were wearing metallic bras underneath gauzy dresses that, come to think of it, looked a lot like the ones Dina and I had had on earlier that day. They were gluing peacock feathers to their faces for some kind of strange photo shoot in a rain forest. The models were all bitching and complaining about the mosquitoes, but I didn't care. I just needed some background noise.

In fact, I turned the volume up high, filling the house with their whining (the girls', not the mosquitoes'), before heading to the kitchen. When I got there, I washed my fork and drinking glass and set them in the drying rack, then swept the kitchen floor. See? I thought to myself as I emptied the dustpan into the garbage. Easy. I *so* had this running-a-household thing under control.

As a reward for being totally on top of everything, I took a bag of microwave popcorn out of the cupboard and popped it, breathing in the warm, buttery smell. I walked back to the living room where I ate the whole bowl by myself while the twiglike models made pouty lips and posed with chimpanzees.

The host and her assistant—that guy with the jet-black hair and scary-white teeth were critiquing the models on their poses. "She's way too stiff," Scary Teeth was saying. "She looks like a frightened sparrow, not a proud peacock. If she could just relax into the pose . . . *own* the outfit . . . really *become* the bird." Easy for him to say, I thought. I'd bet a hundred dollars nobody had ever made *him* wear a see-through dress before.

I sighed and stared miserably at the TV, shoving handful after handful of popcorn into my mouth. It had been a long, strange day and, try as I might, I couldn't get the image of Matt Love's face out of my mind; or Tabby's. I kept picturing the way she'd walked out of that dressing room. The way she'd reached for his hands and wrapped his arms around her waist, tipping her head back to look into his eyes—like it was the most natural thing in the world—exactly like I used to do.

How could I have been so stupid back then? I wondered. When Matt started flirting with me in chemistry and following me around the school asking me out, I thought he'd singled me out because I was special, because he'd cared about me. When really, all along, I'd been replaceable: just a girl who fit into his arms as well as any other girl would fit. But that was most high school guys for you.

Pretty much anyone who was female, decent looking, and willing would do.

The scared sparrow had stepped aside now, and a new model with shockingly red hair had taken her place. She peeked out from behind a tree with sultry eyes as the cameras flashed, then held one hand up over her mouth in a strange way. "Gorgeous," the host was saying. "She's got it. She has so much confidence. She makes peacock look sexy." Seriously? Except for the hair, I couldn't tell the difference between her and the last girl, but then, what did I know about modeling, or anything, really? Maybe there *was* something I was missing; some crucial difference between the sexy peacock and the scared sparrow—between Tabby and me—some very obvious (to everyone else) reason why Matt Love loved her, but didn't love me. She just *had it*. I just didn't.

Well, big deal! I clicked the TV off and carried the popcorn bowl to the kitchen. So what if I didn't have it? If being a sexy peacock was what attracted guys like Matt Love, maybe I was better off being a scared sparrow, anyway. I had other things to focus on, I decided, as I came back to the living room and gathered up my school books.

And, as for Patrick, and his inexplicable crush on me, he'd survive. Give him a week, or a couple of days, even. He'd see that there was nothing special about me. And then he'd be willing to take the next decent-looking girl who came along. . . . And so much the better if that decent-looking girl just happened to be Dina.

In fact, it seemed like he was already getting over it. All things considered, he'd been remarkably chill during our driving lesson. He'd even had me pull into a drive-through where he'd ordered fries. While we'd waited our turn in the line of cars, he'd gathered up the dead roses and casually climbed out to toss them into a nearby trash can. "I don't get why girls like flowers so much, anyway," he'd said when he returned. "They kind of stink." And, because I was still feeling bad about rejecting him, I didn't say a word about the fact that they only stank because they were dead, or about the greasy fries smell that soon filled the car, mixing with the lingering dead roses stench to form a supersmell that was easily ten times worse.

When we got home, he'd even offered to help me shovel the walkway, which was gallant of him and everything, but totally unnecessary. He had his own to do, after all. "What? You think I can't lift a little snow?" I'd said. Then I'd done it myself, working extra-fast so I'd finish ahead of him. "Night," I'd said casually, tossing the shovel into a snowbank, my muscles already burning.

It was 9:30 now, and what had started out as a vague muscle pain had turned into a full-fledged throbbing. I tried to stretch out my shoulders, but it didn't do much good, so I decided to take a hot shower instead before heading to bed. But, first, true to my word, I did the rounds of the house, checking that all the doors and windows were locked. I started in the basement with the small sliding windows—stepping around the giant wardrobe, which was still lying facedown on the floor. It was creepy being down there alone at night, so I worked quickly, switching on all the lights first to reassure myself that there weren't any monsters or bad guys hiding in the corners behind the cardboard boxes and bags of lawn fertilizer. Then I switched them all off again, feeling like a baby for being freaked out enough to check in the first place. I worked my way upstairs from there, checking the ground-floor windows and doors and even making sure that all the burners on the stove—which I hadn't even used—were shut off. Then, reassured that the house was safe and secure and that my paranoid mother would be proud, I went upstairs, showered, and went to bed.

It wasn't until I woke up at three thirty A.M. that I knew something was wrong. My first clue was the fact that I was awake at all. I'm usually a really sound sleeper. My second clue was my nose: It was numb.

I pulled an arm out from underneath my duvet, then quickly pulled it back in again. The air was the temperature of a chilly fall day. My first instinct was to curl up in a ball for warmth, and try to go back to sleep. But, then, that wasn't an option. The house was my responsibility. Forcing myself out of bed, I stumbled over to the radiator and lay my hand on it. That's when I knew for sure that I was screwed. It was three thirty in the morning, in February. I was completely alone, and the furnace was broken.

I grabbed my robe from the hook on the door, stuffed

my feet into a pair of slippers, and went downstairs. "Furnace, furnace, furnace," I muttered, scanning the three-page note my mother had left on the kitchen table. It listed numbers to call and procedures to follow in the event of any and all emergencies. If the key got stuck in the lock, I was supposed to call Jay at LockWorks. If a light burned out, I'd find bulbs under the sink. If my toast was too dark, I should turn the setting to "light." My mother had thought of everything, really. Everything *except* what to do if the furnace died.

I sighed as I switched on the light at the top of the basement stairs. If I was lucky, the furnace would turn out to be one of the many appliances my mother had attached a sticky note to, like the one on the fridge: "If freezer leaks, defrost," or the one on the blender: "Close lid firmly before blending." I wasn't lucky. The furnace had no such helpful sticky note.

My next stop was the computer where I Googled "Furnace Repair, Middleford." Five company sites came up. Only one of them—Hot Stuff Furnace Repair—offered twenty-four-hour service. I dialed the number. The phone rang five times before someone picked up.

"Yeah, what?" a woman's voice answered groggily. I guess you couldn't really expect stellar customer service at that hour of the morning.

"Um. Hi," I said, suddenly feeling like I was ten years old. "Sorry if I woke you up. My name is Elyse. And my furnace is broken. Is this the right number?"

I could hear bed springs creaking. "Dan," the woman shouted, obviously trying to wake her husband. "Danny. A broken furnace."

"You can come?" I said, relief washing over me.

"Sure we can. Where you located?" I gave the woman my address. "You understand," she went on, seeming more awake now that it was time to talk cash, "we charge an up-front service fee of one hundred and seventy-nine dollars for an after-hours emergency call. And the rate is seventy-five dollars an hour after that, plus whatever's needed in parts." I gulped.

"A hundred and seventy-nine dollars? Just to show up?"

"Cash is best. Check is fine, too."

"I'm sorry," I said, my voice going small. "My mom's out of town. I can't write a check. I don't even know if we can afford that."

The woman sighed, like my existence was annoying her. "Well, if you can hold on till morning, the daytime price drops. Seventy-nine for the service call and sixty an hour after that."

"All right," I said. "Sure." I could pay the $79 with my last paycheck, and if I was lucky, it would be a small repair that I could cover with the emergency money my mom had left. She wouldn't even have to know about it until she got home.

The furnace woman told me a few things I should do in the meantime, like turning on a tap and letting it drip so the pipes wouldn't freeze. Then she said they'd be by in the morning. I hung up and hugged my bathrobe tightly around me. The house seemed to be getting colder by the second. I thought about calling my aunt Sarah, to see if I could stay there, but she was all the way across town, and I didn't want to wake her up. Plus, if I called her, she'd make me call my mom, and that was the last thing I wanted. I'd told my mom I could handle taking care of the house on my own, and I intended to do it.

I glanced out the side window—toward Patrick's house—on my way back up the stairs. He'd probably let me in if I knocked on the door, get me some blankets, and let me sleep on the couch, but how weird would that be? I liked him. We were friends. But I'd only known him a week. Plus, I'd just rejected him that afternoon.

So, instead, I went to my mom's room, pulled her bathrobe on, on top of mine, then scrounged around in the linen closet looking for the electric heating pad I used for period cramps. I plugged it into the power outlet in my room, arranged it near my feet, pulled the blankets over my head, and went back to sleep.

And when the sun came up the next morning, things looked better. Sure, the house felt like the inside of a refrigerator, but I was handling it. I had my mom's biggest, warmest coat on and a fleece-lined hat. The repair guys would be there soon. All I had to do was make myself a mug of hot chocolate, curl up with the heating pad, and wait. So I waited. And waited. And waited. When nine o'clock came around, I called school to explain why I wouldn't be in. At ten, I called Hot Stuff Furnace Repair to see how soon they'd be there. The same woman answered.

"Sometime between ten thirty and four," she said.

At first I thought she was kidding. "But I can't wait here all day. You've got to understand. My house is *really* cold right now."

"That happens when the furnace breaks," she answered drily. "Have you got a space heater?" No, I did not have a space heater. Also, I hated her. I hated her with every icy bone in my body. "The guys'll be there as soon as they can. Maybe before noon." But "as soon as they can" didn't end up being before noon at all. At three, I called Mr. Goodman to tell him I'd probably be late for my shift at the store. At four I realized I wouldn't be making it in at all. I called Dina to give her an update and to ask her to tell Patrick I might have to cancel our driving lesson. Then I called Hot Stuff again. Apparently, it was a big day for furnace failure. They'd *probably* be by between six and nine P.M.

After I hung up, I sighed and turned off the TV. I couldn't stand watching another game show, or drinking another mug of hot chocolate, anyway. I figured I might as well go next door to wait for Patrick so I could officially cancel our driving lesson in person. I'd leave a note on the door for the repair guys, telling them where I was. Plus, while I waited, I might actually get warm.

When I got to Patrick's I knocked firmly on the door and waited a minute, then two. I knocked again. Finally, I heard the shuffling of feet. "Hello?" An old man opened the door and stared out at me with big, round eyes. "I thought I heard someone knocking." He smiled. "Are you here to collect for the food bank? I think we've got some tinned pears, but you'll just have to let me see."

"No," I said. "I'm Elyse. From next door."

"What's that?" He leaned forward. "You want more?" He scratched at his head. "Well, I suppose I might have a jar of unopened peanut butter, too. And I've got pickles. Could you use pickles? A big jar of dills, but they're in the cold cellar behind some boxes. If you don't mind coming in and waiting for my grandson to get home, he can carry them up for you."

"Oh, no," I said very loudly. "No pickles. I'm from next door." I pointed toward my house. Then I pointed at myself. "Elyse. Elyse Ulrich. You've met my mom."

"Oh. The Ulrich girl," he said, figuring it out. "You'll have to forgive me. I haven't got my hearing aid in. Come. Come inside. What can I do for you?"

I explained then, in my loudest voice, about the furnace. He nodded. "Now, you've got a gas-burning furnace over there, if I recall," he said. "Have you checked your pilot light?"

I shook my head. I didn't even know what a pilot light was, let alone if our furnace had one. "Well, that'd be your first step. Let me see. . . ." He looked down at his watch. "Patrick won't be home for another few minutes. Have a seat." He motioned toward the living room. "I'll just get my hearing aid in, then I'll be right down. Go over and see if I can have a look for you."

I didn't know if it was the fact that my tear ducts were thawing out after a long, frozen day, the exhaustion from sleeping so badly the night before, or the fact that when he didn't even know who I was, Patrick's grandfather was willing to give me a jar of pickles, but his kindness suddenly overwhelmed me. "Thank you," I said, tears springing to my eyes. I blinked them back. "That would be great." He shuffled up the stairs. While I waited, I took off my boots, wandered into the living room, and sat down, pulling off my mittens and looking around.

The sofa I was sitting on was formal and uncomfortable. Its floral pattern competed with another on the heavy curtains and a third on the wallpaper. Two ceramic lamps flanked it on either side, sitting primly on side tables that hadn't been dusted in months. A collection of Royal Doulton figurines of ladies in ball gowns danced, each frozen midstep, in a dark wood display case. Everything about the place made it obvious that a woman had once loved this room.

I stood up and walked over to the fireplace mantel, which was filled with framed photos that seemed to go in chronological order from left to right. A young bride and her husband standing by a tree, grinning at each other. A shot of the same couple in a park in sepia tones: This time the woman hugged a young child from behind; the man held a baby in his arms. I moved down the line until I got to the ones that showed the couple with silver hair, cuddling two little boys—one with Patrick's curly hair—sitting on the front steps of the same house I was in now.

Patrick's grandmother wore the same smile in each of the photos. Her head tilted slightly to one side, her eyes gleaming with laughter. I walked back down the line of photos, looking at her more carefully as she got younger and younger. She was beautiful, actually, and not just because her hair fell in perfect ringlets and her cheekbones were high. There was an unmistakable warmth and playfulness about her. Plus, it was obvious to me now where Patrick got his twinkly green eyes and curly hair.

I had just reached the last photo again—the wedding photo—when I heard the front door open. "Hi, Grandpa," Patrick said loudly. "I'm home." I was about to call out to let him know I was there, but something caught my eye. I stepped closer to the picture. There, around Patrick's grandmother's neck was a small, heart-shaped pendant. The picture was in black-and-white, so it was hard to tell for sure, but it looked familiar: a lot like the opal pendant my mother had found between the floorboards in our attic the week before. Could it be?

"Well now." I heard Patrick's grandfather's feet on the stairs again. "There he is. Patrick, the Ulrich girl is here, waiting in the living room. Having some trouble with the furnace. I was just about to head over to check on the pilot light."

"I'll do it, Grandpa," Patrick answered. I sighed silently. It was one thing having Patrick's grandfather help with the furnace, but the last thing I wanted was to accept Patrick's help. Even though we'd agreed to be friends, things were bound to still be a bit awkward between us. But also, if he could fix it at all—which was unlikely—the fact that he'd rescued me was bound to go straight to his head. And, if he couldn't—and if he was anything like any other guy I'd ever met—the second blow to his pride would be too much to take.

"There's a good boy," his grandpa said. "Save me going out in the snow. I'll get you my tool belt." A minute later, Patrick's head poked into the living room.

"Patrick-the-furnace-repair-guy, at your service," he said. I gave him a tight smile. "Well, sort of at your service," he continued. "On one condition."

"What's that?" I asked, turning away from the photo and putting my mittens back on.

"As soon as I fix it, we go driving. Dina told me you wanted to cancel, but we've only got seven days left. You're *not* failing that test on my watch."

"You seem pretty confident there," I countered.

"About the driving test or the furnace?"

"Both."

"Yeah. Well, I'm just that good," he said. I rolled my eyes.

But as it turned out, he'd taken an elective in appliance repair back at his school in Toronto, and he *was* that good.

Five minutes later, he was stepping around the giant wardrobe that lay facedown in the middle of our basement floor. "Do you guys always keep that there?" he asked, giving it an odd look.

"Not really." I explained about it falling on my mom. Patrick offered to help me push it upright, but I just shivered and suggested we had bigger, colder problems to focus on at the moment.

He nodded and shone a flashlight into the dark, cobwebby recesses of our basement. "Well, it's not your pilot light," he said, crouching down near the furnace.

"I knew it," I answered. "There's something seriously wrong with this thing. It just completely died. You're not going to be able to fix it. Don't worry. I already called the repair people. They'll be here between six and nine. We'll drive tomorrow. No big deal."

"Hey, not so fast." He held up a hand. "I'm not done." He walked around to the other side of the furnace, resting his hand against this pipe, then that one, hemming and hawing. "Huh," he said finally, a smile breaking across his face. "I think I see your problem."

"You do?"

I watched as he reached up to the ceiling and flicked on a switch—one of the same ones, I realized, I'd flicked off the night before, when I'd been turning off lights after checking that the windows were locked. The furnace hummed to life. Even in the freezing cold basement, I felt the warm flush going to my cheeks.

"You know," he said, "if you really wanted to see me, you could have just come over. You didn't have to shut your furnace off and pretend it was broken. I mean, fake Lyme disease is one thing, but this . . ."

"Look. I didn't. I just—I didn't know what that switch was for. I honestly thought it was broken. And I made it pretty clear yesterday. I don't feel that way about you—I—"

"Relax," he said, giving me a condescending smile. "I was just kidding. Joking? Joshing? Fooling around? Ever heard of it? Plus, I don't feel that way about you either. Not anymore. You don't have to worry. My crush on you is ancient history."

I exhaled heavily, feeling like an egotistical jerk, yet again. Of course he'd just been kidding. I'd given him the brush-off in a pretty serious way the day before and he wasn't stupid. Obviously Patrick didn't have feelings for me anymore. Why would he?

"So, damsel in distress," he said, ignoring the pained look on my face and punching me lightly on the arm. "You ready to drive?"

Chapter 11

Thankfully after rushing, unbidden, to my rescue and restoring heat to my house, Patrick seemed to know enough not to tease me about it during our driving lesson. I mean, seriously, who *hasn't* mistaken a furnace shut-off switch for a light switch at least once in their life? Okay, so maybe I was the only person in the history of the world, but it was an easy enough mistake to make. The idiot who had built the house could have at least made the switches different colors, or labeled them—and that was when I remembered: I knew the idiot who had built the house. Or, at least, I knew who he had been. Patrick had mentioned it during our very first driving lesson.

His grandfather had lived next door since he was a child. *His* father (Patrick's great-grandfather) had built both houses. Of course, that would have been years and years ago. The furnace had probably been replaced since then—so I couldn't really blame Patrick and his relatives for my stupid mistake. Still though, the fact that Patrick's great-grandfather had built the house must have somehow explained how the heart-shaped necklace had ended up in our attic.

Later that night, in my blissfully warm bedroom, I plugged my iPod into its dock and listened to "Gloria"—which had been stuck in my head ever since I'd heard it in Patrick's kitchen. I danced around, flinging socks out of my way, as I sorted through the laundry basket looking for the old jeans I'd been wearing four days ago when my mom and I had unpacked the last of the boxes. When I found them, I took the small pendant out of the pocket and danced downstairs to the sink where I poured chalky white silver polish onto a rag and set to work. I did the chain first, working methodically down the delicate links until the black tarnish had lifted away to reveal gleaming silver. Then I turned my attention to the pendant. It was tiny—no bigger than the fingernail on my pinkie—and it wasn't until I'd rubbed off the last of the tarnish and brought it under the light to examine it that I noticed what had looked like an anchor to hold the stone in was actually a very small diamond. I flipped it over. Some tiny script on the back caught my eye. *MBW took AC. 23-3-1917.* I studied the inscription. Was MBW a person? And, if so, where did he or she take AC? The last initial, I realized, could stand for "Connor"—which was Patrick's grandfather's last name. But, then, the date made no sense. March 23, 1917. I did the math in my head. The pendant was nearly a hundred years old! Patrick's grandfather couldn't have been older than eighty-five. I let it dangle from my hand for a minute, watching it catch the light.

As I walked into the living room the music on my iPod

upstairs changed to a slow romantic song by Eric Clapton, "Wonderful Tonight." It's about an old married couple, and how the man still loves the woman and thinks she's beautiful after all those years. . . . It always made me kind of sad, actually, because in real life, that was almost never how it happened. Just take my parents for example . . . as the years went on, my dad didn't think my mom got more wonderful. He just got bored of her and started cheating. Or take Matt Love. It had only been a matter of months before he'd decided I wasn't worth his time. It was what all men did if you gave them half the chance. Still, the idea behind the song was romantic, and for no good reason, my heart started pounding as I turned the pendant over in my hand. I opened the clasp and held it up to my neck, then went to look at myself in the mirror over the fireplace. The chain was just the right length for me, and the iridescent aqua color of the stone brought out the subtle flecks of blue in my mostly brown eyes. I fastened the clasp and lay my hand over the stone, loving how cool the tiny opal felt against my palm. One thing was for sure: If it *did* belong to Patrick's grandmother, I had to give it back to Mr. Connor. It would be wrong not to. Patrick had said that his grandma died of a stroke recently, which meant his grandparents had been married right up until the end. A love like that was incredibly rare, and I was certain Mr. Connor would want the necklace back. I took my hand away and looked at my reflection again. I would take the pendant next door, I decided, first thing in the morning. Or, better yet, I'd give it to Patrick when I saw him the next afternoon—let him be the one to enjoy the look that would cross his grandfather's face when he saw it again after who knew how many years.

The Eric Clapton song ended, and I reached around my neck to take the opal heart off, then thought better of it. It was nearly a hundred years old, after all. A family heirloom. It would probably be safest if I kept it on. That way I'd be sure not to lose it.

"That's a gorgeous necklace," Dina said right away when she saw me at school the next day.

"Oh, thanks." I glanced up from the lunch table where I was busy cramming for my chemistry test next period. "It's an heirloom," I added for no reason. Obviously, I couldn't mention that it belonged to Patrick's family. I had exactly forty minutes to perfect my understanding of kinetic molecular theory. I didn't have time to tell her the whole story, and I didn't want her jumping to the wrong conclusion—that Patrick had given it to me.

"How was everything at the store yesterday?" I asked instead as I underlined the definitions of heat and temperature change in my notebook.

"Awesome," she answered. Her friends Carly and Cara joined us with their lunch trays. "Even working alone, I still managed to give out some free chocolates and sign fifteen more people up for the customer loyalty program. That makes fifty-six in total. We're more than halfway there!"

Dina's pocket buzzed. She stood up, taking out her phone.

"Is it Patrick?" I asked casually as she read the text.

She shook her head and closed the phone quickly. "Just my mom asking what I want for dinner." She slid it back into her pocket. "I'll write back later."

Carly dipped a fry in some ketchup. "Your mom knows how to text?" she said, obviously impressed. I was, too, to tell the truth. My mom still had trouble working the voice mail on her cell phone. Sometimes she even needed help with the remote control for the TV.

"She took a class," Dina said simply, then changed the subject. "Anybody want this muffin? I'm so full."

"No thanks," I said, absentmindedly putting a hand up to the necklace to check that it was still there—something I'd caught myself doing I don't know how many times that day.

When we got to the store that afternoon, Mr. Goodman was reviewing our customer loyalty stats. He patted us both on the back with his meaty hands. "There are my top salesgirls," he said warmly. "Whatever you're doing, keep it up. Fifty-six customer loyalty cards in two days? Now that's impressive. Sales are up fifteen percent from last week. Fifteen percent!" he repeated, clearly awed. We both smiled and shrugged.

Whether it was because of our stellar sales skills, our sort-of-stolen chocolates, or just the fact that Valentine's Day was fast approaching, the store definitely *was* busier than usual. We were run off our feet most of the shift. Three different times, Dina's phone buzzed in her pocket with a text, but she didn't even have time to answer it. "You should never have let your mom take that texting class," I said when it buzzed the fourth time.

"I know, right?" Dina sighed dramatically. "Now she can contact me twenty-four-seven. Can you cover the cash for a few minutes? I'll just tell her I want fettuccine Alfredo for dinner so she'll leave me alone."

I'd barely punched in my login ID when I looked up and saw a familiar face. "Mrs. Conchetti!" I greeted my favorite customer. "Back for more cards? You'll have that Cupid in time for your grandson's birth for sure. How many days left until your daughter-in-law is due? You must be getting so excited."

"Well," she said, reaching into her purse for her wallet. "Sometimes these things don't happen quite according to plan." She pulled out a wallet-sized photo of a tiny baby and held it out to me, her hand shaking. It was obvious right away that something was wrong, and not only because of the tremor in her hand. The baby in the photo was wearing a tiny oxygen mask. "He was born last Tuesday," she said. "Two weeks premature, which is why I haven't been in until now. They've named him Nolan Conchetti. Five pounds four ounces. The most beautiful baby I've ever seen." I looked up at Mrs. Conchetti. A tear was running down her cheek. "The next day, they diagnosed him with a congenital heart defect—a hole in his heart. He's scheduled for surgery a week from today. He's just so tiny," she said, sliding the photo back into her wallet. She wiped at her cheek with the back of her hand, then ran a pinkie under her eye to clear away her smudged makeup. "Look at me. I'm a mess."

"That's okay, Mrs. Conchetti. Anybody would be. I'm so sorry. I wish there was something I could do." I meant it, but even as I said the words, I knew how hollow they sounded. After all, what could I possibly do to help a sick baby? I glanced down at her purchase: a single card with a kitten dangling from a tree. *Hang in there.*

"For my daughter-in-law," Mrs. Conchetti explained. "I thought this might remind her to keep her chin up. Nolan's a fighter. I can just tell. All the Conchetti men are." I rang up her purchase, then stamped the customer loyalty card she slid across the counter. She was still nine cards short of earning a Cupid doll.

"I don't know why I bothered to get that stamped, considering the circumstances," she said, putting the card back into her wallet. "I don't think I'll be buying enough cards this week to get Nolan the Cupid doll." She sighed. "And I guess the promotion will be over by the time I'm in again. But next year. I'll get it for him next year." She said it like she needed to convince herself that there *would* be a next year for her grandson.

"Of course you will. Next year. Like you said, he's a fighter, right?" She nodded. "You hang in there too," I said, giving her hand a quick squeeze when I passed her her bag. "Let me know how little Nolan is doing whenever you get the chance, okay? I'll be thinking of him."

"Thank you, Elyse. I'll keep you posted," she answered,

smiling bravely before turning to leave. I took a deep breath and tried to blink back my own tears as I sorted the change she'd given me into the cash register.

"Hey, Elyse." I looked up. Patrick was standing beside the counter. How long had he been there? I'd been so focused on Mrs. Conchetti that I hadn't even noticed him coming in. I sighed. I didn't know why—I'd only met her three months ago when I'd started working at Goodman's—but the news about Mrs. Conchetti's grandson being sick had made me really sad. I needed a minute to pull myself together, but that obviously wasn't going to happen with Patrick staring at me.

"Please don't tell me you need another pen," I said. I opened the drawer under the cash and pretended to be looking for something so I wouldn't have to make eye contact. I was too afraid I was about to start crying about the sick baby and I did *not* want him trying to comfort me on top of everything else.

"No," he answered, biting at his lip and shaking his head. "No pen today. Just some cards. But you stay there. It's cool. I can find them myself." He wandered away, thankfully leaving me a few minutes to myself. He came back five minutes before our scheduled driving lesson, dumped an armload of Valentine's Day cards on the counter, then pulled out his wallet, counting out the bills and coins.

"I've got forty-five dollars and seventeen cents," he said finally, sliding the cash and his customer loyalty card toward me. "How many of these can I afford?"

"You'll have to leave these five behind," I said after

I'd totaled up the purchase. "But that still makes eleven cards. Have you met a lot of new girls recently, or something?" I hadn't missed noticing that the card I'd suggested he buy the other day—the blank one with the silver background and red heart—wasn't in the pile. But the nauseating one with the puppies wearing floppy hats (which always made Dina go "Awwwwww") was.

"Hey, it never hurts to be prepared, right?" But I couldn't even force a smile in response to his lame joke. He'd just gone and proven to me what I'd suspected all along: Like most guys his age, Patrick wasn't picky. I'd turned him down, so he was moving on without a backward glance. He'd be covering his bases by giving tons of valentines to tons of girls; then he'd be happy with whoever took him up on his offer.

Dina, who was standing near the printer paper texting her mom again, looked up and waved at him. I felt my heart sink. I knew that she had a serious crush on him, but if this was the way Patrick was going to be, by encouraging her to pursue him, was I just setting her up to get her heart broken?

The thought distracted me all through my driving lesson that afternoon. "So, are those cards for girls at your school?" I asked Patrick after I'd steered the car onto the highway ramp for high-speed-merging-hell, part two. "Or will you mail them to girls back home in Toronto?" I pressed when he didn't answer.

He fiddled with the CD player. Today's driving soundtrack wasn't Surely Sarah, but it was similar. Soft and acoustic, but with a male lead singer this time.

"I haven't exactly decided yet," he answered. "You're going to want to get into the left-hand lane here." I checked my mirror and blind spot, then quickly glanced over at Patrick before changing lanes. He was gazing out the window nonchalantly.

"What do you mean 'you haven't decided'?" I said. "It's almost Valentine's Day. And, in case you don't know, you're supposed to have *one* valentine. Not eleven. It's not the time to be keeping your options open."

"Why not?" he asked. "Our exit is the one after this. Start moving to the right."

"Why did you make me move to the left in the first place, then?" I asked, irritated. I checked my blind spot again and, as I did, caught a glimpse of Patrick grinning like an idiot. "Because it's not romantic to have eleven valentines. It's like you're telling every one of those girls how unspecial they are to you." He seemed to think about that for a few minutes.

"There's our exit," he said finally. "Get ready to pull off, then let's try to find a space to practice parking." He took his hat off and scratched his head, then wriggled out of his jacket. For once, the car heater actually seemed to be working. As he stuffed his coat into the backseat, it was impossible not to notice the way it smelled, even though it took me a few seconds to figure out what it was. A not altogether unappealing mixture of coffee, sawdust, and engine grease—probably picked up from the shops at his school, Middleford Tech. I signaled and pulled onto the off-ramp. "You wouldn't just happen to be jealous, would you?" he asked.

"And why would I be jealous?"

"Because you don't think you're in my top eleven."

I snorted. "Right, because that would be such an honor." The second I'd said it, I knew it sounded mean. After all—even if by now it was "ancient history"—he *had* confessed a crush on me just a few days before.

"Hey," he shot back. "Some girls would be honored. I've had girlfriends before, you know?" he added, sounding almost hurt. "Lots of them. And, anyway, I didn't say I *wasn't* getting you a valentine. You can be number twelve if you want."

Now I didn't care if I sounded mean. "Awesome. I'll wait for my card with bated breath." I turned the wheel sharply to the left. A little too sharply, probably. We came around the corner in a skid. Patrick grabbed the wheel and steered us back on course. "Sorry," I said. Driving and being irritated with Patrick were two things that obviously didn't mix well. I knew I should change the subject to something safer. My first thought was the necklace, but I quickly decided against it. It was a precious heirloom, after all. A symbol of lasting love. Any guy who bought eleven valentines and bragged about how many girlfriends he'd had didn't deserve to touch it. I'd just give it to his grandfather when we got home.

"How's your songwriting going?" I asked instead, as I calmed myself down and accelerated gently. I hadn't asked him about it since the first day I'd officially met him, when he bought pen number one.

Now it was his turn to get flustered. He shrugged and looked out the window. "Okay."

"Just okay? You know, if you're ever looking for someone to play for, I wouldn't mind listening to one of your songs."

"Yeah. I don't know about that," he said. "I don't really sing in front of people, besides my friend Jax."

"How are you ever going to be a famous singer-songwriter, then? And what about your band? You'll never make it to the top of the charts if you don't perform. You know, you just need to work on your confidence," I said, repeating one of the aggravating things he'd said to me during our first driving lesson. "I'm sure you're awesome. Plus," I went on, "most girls are totally into that kind of thing. If you want to impress the top eleven . . ." I trailed off, but, obviously, I was thinking of Dina. If he sang her a song he'd written himself, she'd melt into a puddle of girl-goo.

"Oh my God," I said, suddenly coming up with a brilliant plan. "You should write a song for Dina's party." He looked at me uncertainly. "It could be, like, your big debut. In front of a real audience." Just the idea made him turn about two shades paler than usual. "Think of it as extreme songwriting. Do this, and you'll never be afraid to sing in front of people again. Come on." I grinned, knowing I had him. "I dare you. Unless, of course, you're too scared."

That sealed the deal. No guy would admit to being too scared. "All right," he said, gulping. "You're on. Just be prepared to be blown away."

"Oh, I'm prepared," I said, slowly pulling ahead. I braked gently, threw the car into reverse, then carefully maneuvered into a space between a minivan and a hatchback.

"Because, when I'm done singing," he went on, obviously trying to gather his courage, "every girl at the party is going to be begging to be let into my top eleven. You might even have to fight to hold on to your spot at number twelve."

Without thinking, I raised one hand to my chest, laying it over the heart pendant again. Then I put the car back into drive, checked my blind spot, and pulled out of the space. "Well," I answered. The words came out of my mouth in a flirty tone I hadn't at all intended. "I guess we'll see. If your songs are really that good, I just might want to hold on to that spot."

"Keep parking like that," Patrick said, motioning toward the empty space I'd just left behind, "and I just might bump you up to number eleven. That was awesome." I felt a strange, unexpected gush of pride and gratitude at his words. Not because I was aiming to be Patrick's number eleven—obviously—but because he was right, I had just parallel parked, all by myself, and I'd done it without even hyperventilating or swearing. In truth, I'd barely even had to think about it. Clearly, a miracle had just taken place.

"Thanks," I said simply, and still smiling, I turned the car toward home.

Chapter 12

The only downside to doing my very first independent parallel park that day turned out to be coming back to an empty house and having no one to tell. "Guess what?" I said to the many stuffed pandas my mom had dug out from the basement before leaving for Mexico. She'd even washed them and lined them up on my desk in preparation for Dina's party. "I parked!" I picked one up and squished its soft black-and-white head. It looked back at me blankly.

I flopped down on the bed, hugging it happily to my chest anyway. Maybe it was just because I was on top of the world from the whole parking thing, but I suddenly wasn't anticipating Dina's party—or Valentine's Day, really—with the same amount of dread. Not only was I going to get to see how happy it made Dina to adopt not one but two endangered bears, but I'd also get to watch Patrick sing in front of an audience for the first time. Somehow, I doubted he'd have all the girls swooning and fainting around his feet like he planned, but, at the very least, Dina would be impressed.

Plus, he'd get a chance to really see her in action—making everyone feel welcome at her party while she saved the world one bear at a time. How could he not be impressed enough to forget about the rest of his top eleven and focus on her instead? Getting to sit back and watch it happen—knowing I'd orchestrated the whole thing—might even be kind of fun.

The next morning was Saturday, and I wasn't scheduled to start my shift at work until two. I slept until ten, then spent another hour lounging around in bed reading. By the time I finally made it downstairs, I was starving. I reached for the Cheerios and went to pour them into a bowl. A small handful fell out, followed by that bottom-of-the-box Cheerio dust. I sighed, threw the box out, put the milk carton (which was also nearly empty) back in the fridge, and reached for the bread, figuring I'd have toast instead. But the second I touched the bag, I could tell the loaf was stale. Obviously there was a reason my mother always put the twist tie back on right away and stored the loaf in the bread box—both things I hadn't bothered to do after breakfast the morning before, despite the helpful sticky note on the bread box that instructed me to do so.

I went back upstairs to get dressed, glancing at the opal pendant, which was sitting on my dresser. It wasn't that I'd *exactly* forgotten to give it back to Patrick's grandfather the day before. It was just that, by the time Patrick and I had pulled into the driveway after my lesson, this really goofy song was playing on the car stereo, and Patrick was doing a bongo solo on his own head, which was too geeky for words, and really made me doubt his story about having loads of girlfriends back in Toronto (he'd probably just said it to save his pride). And then he'd started playing bongos on my head, too, and all in all, the moment just hadn't felt quite right for the return of long-lost heirlooms. I was planning to go over to give it back to Mr. Connor soon, though. Probably even that day. Just not right that second. First, I had to concentrate on getting showered and dressed. My leisurely morning was over. I needed to go grocery shopping.

I had to admit I felt pretty mature when I stepped off the number eight bus and walked across the parking lot of ValuePlus Grocery half an hour later. All around me were families loading bags of food and cases of pop into their cars, old ladies dragging bundle buggies full of soup and canned tuna, and even one or two college students who didn't look much older than me sauntering in with reusable bags thrown over their shoulders. I swung my own canvas bag on my arm, all cool and collected. That is, until I got into the store.

Obviously, I'd been grocery shopping with my mother a trillion times. I knew where the carts were, and how to pull one free from the row. I could probably have found my way to the milk and bread aisles blindfolded. It was just that I'd never been there by myself before, with money in my pocket, and nobody to tell me what to buy.

I started out with the best of intentions, picking out

three bananas and a very responsible head of lettuce. But that got me thinking about Caesar salad with creamy dressing and homemade croutons. I'd seen a crouton recipe in one of my mom's magazines a while back that looked pretty easy. I'd need a loaf of French bread, garlic, parsley, and Parmesan cheese. But, since this was going to be a seriously fancy salad, I didn't want the cheap stuff in the can. I headed for the real Parmesan at the deli counter. My jaw dropped when I saw the price: $12.75! For cheese! I threw it in the cart anyway. After all, it was for salad. My mother would approve.

I sailed through the chips and pop aisle unscathed, and barely glanced at the ice cream. It was the baking section that was my downfall. I needed stuff for the pinwheel cookies and cheesecake I'd promised Dina, so I piled in a bag of flour, a pound of sugar, cocoa, vanilla, and a huge bag of semisweet chocolate chunks. Then I noticed these adorable paper liners for muffin cups that had tiny hearts on them, and if I was going to make muffins, too, I'd need more flour—not to mention eggs, butter, and two packages of cream cheese for the cheesecake. While I was in the dairy aisle, I picked up some milk and some mini fruit bottom yogurts, and then, on impulse, a bag of Oreo cookies the next aisle over. I could use them to make panda decorations on the cake. Dina would die.

"That'll be fifty-two dollars and sixty-five cents," the cashier said after scanning the last bag of flour. I gulped. I'd only been planning to get Cheerios, milk, and bread—so when I'd pulled one $50-bill off the small roll of cash my mother had left for food and emergencies, it had seemed like more than enough. I dug through my pockets for change, trying to ignore the dirty looks from the woman in line behind me. She was flipping impatiently through a *National Enquirer* while she waited to pay for a single jumbo-sized box of Honey Nut Cheerios. And that was when I realized: Cheerios! I'd completely forgotten the Cheerios. I'd also forgotten the bread, unless you counted the baguette I'd picked up for my croutons. Well, there was no going back for them now.

"Um. Sorry," I said, laying out my last pennies on the conveyor belt. "That's fifty-two forty-seven." I shrugged apologetically. "I guess I'll have to put something back. What about the lettuce. How much did it cost again?"

"Oh for Pete's sake," the grouchy tabloid/Cheerios lady said. She slapped twenty cents down on the counter. "Let's just keep the line moving."

"Thanks." I smiled sweetly, hoping she'd chill out. "Thanks a lot. I'll pay you back." It was a stupid thing to say. Obviously, I'd probably never see her again. Even though a huge photo of Angelina Jolie in a bikini was covering most of her face, I could tell she was rolling her eyes at me.

"You want bags?" the cashier asked me, twirling a lock of her hair. "Five cents each."

"No. No thanks." I held up my reusable bag. It wasn't like I had an extra five cents anyway. But, as it turned out, $52.65 worth of groceries didn't fit very well into one bag. I stuffed the chocolate chunks and muffin liners into my coat pockets, and piled a bunch more into the bag. When I was done, the seams looked like they were about to split, and I was still left holding a bag of sugar in the crook of my arm. To make matters worse, it had started to snow again.

No big deal, I reassured myself, lugging the heavy bag across the parking lot. I just had to make it to the bus stop; then I'd be as good as home. And that was when I realized: I'd counted out all of my change onto the conveyor belt. All of it. Including my bus money.

"Stupid, stupid, stupid," I muttered to myself as I started down the sidewalk, snow flying in my face. How could I have possibly been so stupid? Home was at least a twenty-minute walk away, and the strap of the shopping bag was already cutting into my shoulder, making my arm feel all tingly and weird. I looked back at the grocery store. I'd barely made it half a block, and I had at least another twelve to go. I couldn't see any other option.

"Excuse me?" I said, approaching a woman pushing a stroller. "I need to make a phone call. I'm all out of money. Do you have a quarter?" She walked past like she hadn't even heard. "Excuse me?" I tried again, approaching a man who was opening his car. "Do you have a—"

"Sorry," he said, getting in and closing the door before I could even finish my sentence. I bit my lip, fighting back tears. Not only did I suddenly feel helpless and alone, but I also felt guilty, thinking about ice-kicking Jack and all the other street people I'd passed with barely a glance. "Excuse me?" I said softly, this time to an old man. He shuffled past, head bowed against the drifting snow.

Dejected, I let my bag fall to the sidewalk with a thud. I shouldn't have expected anyone to feel sorry for me. I was a healthy, well-dressed teenager carrying an overflowing bag of food. I obviously wasn't in dire need. I took a deep breath, resigning myself to the fact that I had a long, slow, cold walk ahead of me.

"Need a quarter?" somebody asked. I looked up. A guy with a ponytail was holding out his hand. "I heard you asking."

I nearly hugged him. "Thank you," I said, pulling off my mitten to take it. "I bought too much stuff and I ran out of money for the bus. My mom's away in Mexico on this trip, and I don't have a cell phone so I—" He held up his hand to stop me, obviously not interested in my life story.

"Peace," he said instead, holding up two fingers before walking off.

"Peace," I shouted back, eager to thank him. "Peace to you, too. And thanks. Thanks so much. Really."

Hoisting my bag up over my shoulder, and readjusting the sugar in my arms, I made my way toward a phone booth near the bus stop. I pushed the quarter into the slot and dialed, hoping to God the only person I could turn to would answer. The phone rang three times before finally—

"Hello?"

"Dina! Oh, thank God. It's Elyse. I need a favor. I'm outside ValuePlus Grocery. I accidentally spent my bus money. Can you come pick me up? I swear, I wouldn't ask if I had any other way. . . ."

"Oh no," Dina said. "You know I would, but I'm at the salon getting highlights for the party. It's so weird that you called though. I'm on the other line with Patrick. We were just talking about you."

"Really?" I knew they'd exchanged numbers, and that Patrick had called her that one time to pass along the message about his fake Lyme disease, but I hadn't realized they talked regularly. Did this mean what I thought it did? I was just about to ask who had called who first, but then I remembered I only had the one quarter. If my time ran out, I'd be in serious trouble. I could ask her about Patrick later. "How long do you think the highlights are going to take?" I asked instead.

"I don't know. Let me find out." Dina covered the phone with her hand. "The colorist says half an hour to forty-five minutes. But she needs to check it every twenty minutes to make sure. I'm so sorry, Elyse. I can come right after. Can you wait?" The snow was really starting to blow now. I shivered inside the tiny booth as I tried to balance the sugar on top of the phone.

"Sure," I answered. What other choice did I have?

"Or, wait. Oh my God. You're at ValuePlus, right? I'll ask Patrick if he can come get you. He's at the music store on Jones, right up the street. Just a sec."

"Dina, no—" I started, but she'd already clicked over to the other line. I'd rather have frozen. Or dumped the groceries in a snowbank and walked the twelve blocks home. After the whole furnace thing, I *so* didn't need Patrick teasing me about being a "damsel in distress" again.

Dina's voice came back on the line. "He says no problem. Are you at the Laird entrance, or the one on Southvale?"

"It's okay," I said. "Tell him thanks, but I'm just going to wait until your hair is done. I mean, I don't want to inconvenience him."

"But it's really cold out, Elyse," she said reasonably. "And he said it was okay. I can't stand thinking of you outside for the next forty-five minutes. Laird or Southvale?"

"Laird, but—" The phone made its little call-waiting clicky sound again.

A few seconds passed. "Near the corner or the bus stop?" she asked, coming back on the line.

"The bus stop, but, Dina, I *really* don't mind waiting for you—"

"One sec," she interrupted. The phone clicked again. "Okay. He'll be there in two minutes. Clarissa needs to check my highlights. I'd better go. But I'll see you this afternoon at work, okay?"

"Wait—" I went to protest again, but it was too late. She'd already hung up. I sighed as I replaced the receiver, then I struggled through the swinging doors of the phone booth with my humongous grocery bag.

No more than a minute could have passed before the

red car pulled up. Like, what? Had he been sitting in the parking lot with the car idling, just waiting to rush to the rescue? Patrick popped the trunk and hit the four-way flashers, then climbed out and came around to help me. It took every ounce of willpower I had not to glare at him. What did he think this was? Nineteenth-century England? I wasn't some kind of genteel, tea-sipping lady-in-waiting. I'd carried it this far. I could lift the bag of groceries into the car by myself.

"Hey," he called brightly, taking the bag from me without asking and hoisting it into the trunk. "You should have knocked on the door. If I'd known you needed groceries I could have driven you. I was going to RecordRunner anyway."

"I just needed a few things," I answered. He glanced down at the bulging, overflowing shopping bag he'd just lifted. It easily weighed forty pounds. "And, anyway, the bus goes right by." I bit my tongue and forced the next words out. After all, it *was* nice of him to drive me home. "Thanks for coming to get me."

"Yeah, no problem," he said. "Actually, I was glad you called." I clenched my hands into tight fists, determined not to point out that I hadn't, in fact, called him. I'd called Dina, who just so happened to have him on the other line. "Do you have ten minutes to come back to RecordRunner with me? I was just talking to Dina and we couldn't agree on which music we liked. I was trying to play her some tracks over the phone, but she couldn't hear very well with all the hair dryer noise at the salon. I'm helping her put together a playlist for the party," he explained.

"Oh," I said, my mind racing. So *that's* why he'd been talking to Dina. That was good. It meant he and Dina would be spending time on the phone and in person over the next few days . . . talking, bonding, listening to romantic songs together. It couldn't hurt. Maybe, I even let myself speculate, he'd come to pick me up as a favor to Dina. Maybe he *already* liked her and was trying to impress her by looking out for her best friend. My anger at his whole knight-in-shining-armor routine started to melt away. "That's really nice of you to do the music for Dina's party. Sure. I've got time, I guess. I can help."

As soon as we got to RecordRunner, Patrick set to work. He borrowed a stool from one of the cashiers and pulled it up to a listening station for me; then he started lining up the songs on the digital sampling screen. "Okay, here's the deal," he said, standing behind me. I couldn't help noticing how, when he reached out to touch the screen, his arms brushed my shoulders. "I'll play you the first thirty seconds of each one. You say yes or no. We're done in ten minutes." He clapped a pair of giant, puffy earphones over my head and put on a matching set before pulling up a stool beside me, so close our knees almost touched.

"Uh-uh," I said, about ten seconds into the first song. It was some nauseating top-40 thing full of "baby, baby I love you" stuff. "No. No. No." We went through the next three. He vetoed the fourth before I even had the chance.

"Céline Dion should be banned," he said. I laughed.

"I couldn't agree more. Her songs make me want to throw up a little in my mouth. Okay. This one's a yes," I said finally. It was Nat King Cole and his daughter singing "Unforgettable." "Yes again," I said to Van Morrison's "Brown Eyed Girl." "I've always loved this song. I love everything by Van Morrison."

"You like the classics, eh?" Patrick said. "You've got good taste."

I blushed at his compliment, even though it was silly. I mean, *everybody* who's heard "Brown Eyed Girl" likes it.

We both agreed on a few Surely Sarah songs, and a bunch of stuff by the Doors. "You forgot 'Gloria,'" I pointed out as we neared the bottom of the list, reminding him of the song he'd made oatmeal cookies and spatula-danced to. "That's, like, the rock-and-roll anthem of all time."

He smacked himself on the forehead so hard that he nearly fell backward off his stool. Without thinking, I reached out a hand to steady him. "Thanks," he said, laughing at himself as he sat up straight again. It took me a second to realize that I was still touching him, and I quickly dropped my arm.

"Oh no," I said, turning my attention back to the list of songs on the screen in front of us. "You *do* realize what we've just done, right?" He followed my gaze and scanned the screen. About twenty songs on the list had a red strike through them, to show we'd rejected them, and the genre listed beside almost all of them was "soft rock" or "pop."

"We just took out absolutely every song that Dina requested," he said, his eyes going wide as he got my drift.

"Except that one." I pointed out a lame top-40 love song by a band called SugarPop Baby that we'd somehow forgotten to cut.

"Okay," he said. "How can we fix this?" The look on his face was so sweet; so worried when he thought about hurting Dina's feelings like that I almost wanted to throw my arms around him and hug him for being so thoughtful . . . but, obviously, I restrained myself.

"It's not going to be easy," I said, scanning the list instead, "but we can do this. We just need to pick the least bad ones."

We started at the very first song again, scoring each of them on a scale of one to ten, where tens were decent, if cheesy, and ones were so sappy they might induce involuntary retching.

"Seriously, Britney Spears?" I said when he suggested keeping "E-mail My Heart," a little-known song off her first album.

"Hey," Patrick said, "in case you haven't heard, she's making a comeback. But 'Lady in Red'?" he challenged in return.

"Trust me," I assured him. "Dina loves that song." He hit accept.

Our only real disagreement came when Patrick wanted

to include Phil Collins's "Against All Odds." "We can't," I groaned.

"Why not? Dina put it on the list with a star beside it." He showed me a piece of loose-leaf paper with Dina's unmistakable loopy handwriting on it. The I's were all dotted with little hearts that had smiley faces in them.

"It just . . ." I stalled, not sure what to say. Dina had told me the story a million times about how that song had come on the radio once, and Damien had asked her to slow dance to it even though they were just alone in her bedroom. She always finished by saying it was the sweetest thing ever and she'll always cherish the memory. Usually by the end of retelling it, she'd be wiping tears from her eyes and honking her nose into a Kleenex. But I couldn't tell Patrick that. He might think she was still in love with Damien and lose hope. "It might . . . make her sad," I said. "Because she likes that song, but she'll have nobody to dance with."

Patrick shrugged, like he couldn't figure out what the big deal was. "I'll ask her to dance when it comes on," he said, like it was that simple. And maybe it was. I bit at my lip, not sure why tears had suddenly sprung to my own eyes. I was happy for my friend, after all—for both of my friends. Maybe it was because Patrick was so thoughtful . . . so careful about Dina's feelings and so willing to include the songs she loved on the playlist, even though he hated them. He treated her so differently from the way Matt Love had treated me. Maybe I was just jealous I'd never found that kind of love.

Patrick hit print on the screen and went to collect our list, which thankfully gave me a second to pull myself together; then he was back, gently lifting the earphones off my head.

"Oh God," I said, catching a glimpse of his watch. I grabbed his wrist to make sure. "It's one thirty. I start work at two." I'd already missed a day of work for the furnace that week and been late because of my run-in with Matt Love. If I was late again, Mr. Goodman would officially freak.

"No problem. I'll download the rest. I just want to buy this one." He held up the Van Morrison CD. "Then I'll drop you at work."

"But you're not going that way."

"I'm going to pick up my friend Jax at his house to bring him over for a band rehearsal, and I'm not working today, so not really, but I've got time."

"What about the groceries?"

"Give me your house keys and I'll put them away for you after I get Jax." He saw me hesitate. "You can trust me," he went on. "Plus, if I steal anything, you know where I live, right?" He had a point.

"Okay," I said reluctantly, then added, "thanks."

"Sure," he answered. "I owe you, anyway. If you hadn't been here to help me, I might have bought this one." He held up a Michael Bolton CD.

Obviously, he was kidding. "The top eleven would *not*

have approved," I said, shaking my head at the CD. Even Dina thought Michael Bolton was cheesy, and that was saying something.

"Exactly," he said. "See what I mean?" He put an arm around me. "Lucky thing I've got you on my side." His touch felt familiar and warm and not at all weird. I didn't shrug him off or pull away—but then, I barely had time. A heartbeat later, he'd let go. "Give me a sec," he said.

I watched him at the cash. He talked with his hands, making big gestures in the air as he and the sales guy compared notes about some new release they'd just heard. You could tell just by watching him: He was friendly. A genuinely nice guy when you got right down to it. So, maybe he had a tendency to tease people (or maybe it was just me) a bit too much. And maybe he was playing the field a little by giving out all those valentines, but so what? Once he really got to know Dina, they were going to be perfect for each other. He was considerate, too, which was something Dina deserved after putting up with oops-I-got-drunk-and-didn't-return-your-call-for-sixteen-hours Damien. Patrick knew I was in a rush, so he only talked to the cashier for a minute. Then he turned to me, smiling.

"You driving?" he asked, holding out the car keys.

I reached for the ring, then twirled them around one finger, liking the sound the keys made as they hit against one another—like wind chimes, only solid and practical instead of delicate and sweet. "Sure," I answered. "Why not?"

Chapter 13

It turned out that Patrick had some pretty decent navigation skills. He directed as I drove through alleyways and parking lots most of the way to the mall, avoiding all but one stoplight and making it there with a full five minutes to spare before my shift started. Dina—her hair freshly highlighted and blow-dried straight—pulled into the parking lot right behind us, waving.

"Hey," she called, climbing out of her car. The light reflected off her sleek locks and, with the snow flying all around her, she looked like some kind of Italian ice princess. I didn't miss the fact that Patrick did a double take when he saw her. I tried my best to hang back, lingering near the car door as they talked about the soundtrack for the party.

"That sounds awesome, Patrick," Dina said, batting her big brown eyes as he gave her the rundown of the current playlist. "Oh. And since you're going with mostly older songs, you know what you should add? 'Lady in Red.' My parents danced to it at their tenth anniversary. I think it's *so* romantic." Patrick shot me a quick, almost undetectable look of gratitude from the other side of the car.

"Already on the list," he said, which made her grin and blush like crazy.

After that, the afternoon passed in a blur. Since it was the last weekend before Valentine's Day, the store was packed with people buying sentimental cards and tacky stuffed toys. Using our boxes of somewhat-stolen chocolates, we managed to sign up twenty more people for the customer loyalty program (earning another $100 toward Dina's second panda). Four people even bought enough cards to earn their very own singing Cupids. "We're down to the last five dolls," Dina said after checking the storage room. "At this rate, they'll be gone by tomorrow." If I'd had time, I would have done a happy dance.

By quarter to six, things had slowed down, and even though he wasn't working a shift at the Keyhole, and even though I'd technically already driven that day, Patrick came back to get me for my lesson. When I saw him, I ducked into the back room so he'd have to talk to Dina first. I peeked out the door and, as soon as they looked deep in conversation, snuck back out and pretended to be dusting the Precious Moments shelves one aisle over from the cash. They couldn't see me, but I could hear every word they were saying.

"All right. So, with these four valentines, that makes fifteen cards," Dina said. I could hear the slight sticky sound of the happy face stamp we used as Dina filled in the squares on Patrick's customer loyalty card. "Your total comes to fifteen dollars and seventy-four cents. And this adorable little guy is yours." A Cupid doll started to sing. Dina giggled. "Do you know who you're going to give it to?" she asked.

I could hear the rustling of plastic as Dina bagged his cards. *More* cards! Fifteen valentines in total! Playing the field was one thing, but this was a bit ridiculous, even for Patrick.

"Yeah. I've got someone in mind," he answered. "I think this Cupid is going to make them really happy. Or, I hope so, anyway."

I fumbled with my dust rag, nearly dropping a figurine of two big-headed angels hugging a teddy bear between them. He *had* to be talking about Dina. Nobody else in their right mind would want such an irritating doll.

And if I had any doubts about his feelings for her, they had vanished by the end of our driving lesson that day. The snow that had started while I was grocery shopping was still falling, only now the temperature had gone up a bit, changing the small flakes to wet, sleety stuff that seemed to freeze as soon as it hit the ground. The walk across the parking lot alone was treacherous.

"Maybe we should cancel the lesson for today," I suggested as I held on to the trunk of a parked car to steady myself. Even the talk radio station we listened to in the store was saying that driving conditions were bad and that extreme care should be taken.

"Hey," Patrick answered, taking a running start and

sliding across an icy patch on his boots. "This is nothing. I'm from Canada. This is how we do winter." He slid to a stop, then turned to face me. "You'll have to learn to handle these kinds of road conditions, anyway." I sighed. Clearly I wasn't getting out of driving. "We'll stick to the side streets, okay?" he offered. "We'll take it slow. What if we work on braking?"

"All right," I agreed, getting into the car. After all, when it came to driving, stopping had to be the safest part.

He directed while I drove carefully out of the parking lot and took a left into the small subdivision just behind the mall. Everyone must have been holed up inside to wait out the storm, because the streets were deserted. "All right," Patrick said. "See that stop sign? You're going to want to start braking as smoothly as possible, beginning way back. Slamming on the brakes too soon will make you skid. You can't be too careful when it's icy like this." I tried it. "Good," he said. "You've got it. Just keep practicing."

I signaled right and drove slowly toward the next stop sign. "So?" I said casually as I started to brake again. "Dina's hair looked really great today, didn't it?" Then, so I wouldn't seem too obvious about it all, I added, "Her colorist is supposed to be awesome. I'm making an appointment there, too, I think." We came to a safe stop, and I glanced over to see his reaction. After all, I'd seen his eyes go wide when he'd noticed how beautiful Dina looked. If I could just get him to admit it, I'd know for sure that he liked her.

He shrugged. "I don't know. I don't mind your hair how it is now." He fiddled with the heating vents. "But, yeah. I guess Dina looked really nice today."

I accelerated gently. "I know. But then, she *always* looks really nice."

"Yeah. She's pretty." I spotted another stop sign halfway down the block and headed toward it. Okay, so he liked her hair. He thought she was pretty. This was all good, but it didn't necessarily mean that he liked her, did it? He probably thought lots of girls were pretty. Fifteen girls, to be exact.

There was a blue car coming up behind us now, moving pretty fast. I slowed down even earlier than normal, braking gently like Patrick had taught me, so the driver would see my lights and do the same. I came to a safe stop, then signaled left and started to turn the wheel. I tried to think of a subtle way to find out for sure. After all, Dina would kill me if I let Patrick know she had a huge crush on him.

Turns out I didn't have to worry though. Patrick was one step ahead of me. "Hey," he asked suddenly, "is she single?"

So, he liked her. I had my answer. "Yeah," I replied. I felt a lump rising in my throat for no good reason. "She's single." What was my problem, anyway? I didn't want a boyfriend under any circumstances, plus, I should have been happy for Dina. Patrick was a great guy. She was a great girl. They'd be twice as great together. I glanced in the rearview mirror again to avoid having to look at Patrick. The last thing I needed was for him to notice the devastated look cross my face and to ask what was wrong. I was just blinking back my tears when, out of the corner of my eye, I noticed the blue car that was still coming behind us. *Right* behind us. Before I knew what I was doing, I'd stepped on the gas. Hard. We lurched forward turning left across the intersection.

"Oh God," I said, slamming on the brakes. But the car didn't stop. Somewhere behind us I heard a screeching sound. Our tires spun on a patch of ice and slid sideways. Patrick reached for the wheel to steer us out of the skid, but it was useless. The road was too slick.

"Try shifting into neutral," he shouted. I did. The car slowed, but kept sliding until it stopped with a thud, half the front bumper buried in a snowbank.

"Elyse? Are you okay?" Patrick asked. I was still clutching the steering wheel as if my life depended on it.

"Yeah. You?"

"I'm okay." He glanced back. "God, that was close." I turned to see what he was looking at. Across the street, and about twenty feet back, the blue car that had been following us was up on the curb—inches from a huge tree. "I'll be right back," Patrick said, climbing out of the car. "Hey!" he shouted as he jogged across the street. "You all right in there?"

I covered my mouth with my hand to keep a sob from

escaping. What had I just done? I could have killed us both, not to mention the person in the blue car. I should have been concentrating on driving instead of on my friend's love life and my lack thereof. That was it. I was clearly unfit for the roads.

I looked back again. A man in a trench coat was getting out of the blue car. He and Patrick walked around to the front, checking for damage. I breathed a small sigh of relief. At least the man was walking. He was okay. Nobody had been hurt.

Nodding their heads, they started back toward the red car where I was still sitting, barely breathing. Patrick opened the driver's-side door. "Don't worry. Everyone's okay," he told me. "This is Stu."

"Hi, Stu." I waved weakly. "I'm so sorry."

He didn't seem to hear me, though. "I'm sorry," he said almost at the same time. "I should have been going slower with this black ice. Things could have been a lot worse if you hadn't accelerated and swerved out of the way."

Swerved out of the way? Me? All I'd done was hit the gas, much too hard, and not even on purpose. I'd known the blue car was close behind me and coming pretty fast. But that wasn't why I hit the gas. Or was it?

Stu and Patrick walked around the red car then. "We won't know until we get you out of there," Stu said thoughtfully, "but I don't think there should be much damage."

Twenty minutes later, between a snow shovel the very

resourceful Stu kept in his trunk, some pushing, and a lot of tire spinning, Patrick had managed to back the car out of the snowbank and onto the road. The front was a little dented. Nothing else seemed to be broken, but Patrick and Stu exchanged numbers, just in case.

When we were ready to go, Patrick opened the passenger-side door for me. Obviously, after what I'd just done, I shouldn't have been expecting him to let me drive—and honestly, I didn't *want* to drive—but it stung all the same.

"I'm canceling my road test," I said as soon as we'd started to move.

"What?" He looked over at me.

"I'm dangerous. Look what just happened. I nearly totaled your car."

"Didn't you hear what Stu said?" Patrick asked. "You just saved my car from being rear-ended. I didn't even teach you rear collision avoidance yet." He seemed to be searching his brain. "Did I? You just knew it instinctively. I should be thanking you."

I stared at him incredulously. "No, you shouldn't. You should be furious with me. I nearly killed you." He actually laughed. "Why aren't you mad?" I demanded. The one time Matt Love had let me drive his car I'd accidentally scraped the paint on one of the doors pulling out of the narrow alleyway near his house. He'd nearly had a heart attack.

"Because you're okay. I'm okay. Even the car is more

or less okay. I can hammer those dents out in about two minutes. Hang on," he said, pulling into a McDonald's parking lot. "I'm buying you a milk shake."

"What? Why?" I stared at him.

"To celebrate your awesome winter-driving skills," he answered, "and your upcoming road test. You're going to walk into that panda party on Friday as a licensed driver," he said. "There's no doubt in my mind." He got out and came around to the passenger side. "Come on," he said as he grabbed my hand to pull me out. "Chocolate, vanilla, or strawberry?"

I couldn't understand it. I'd just crashed his car, and he wanted to buy me a milk shake? Was there something wrong with him? Or—the thought suddenly occurred to me—did he still have feelings for me? I pushed the idea away as quickly as it surfaced, though. After all, what had his exact words been in my basement? "My crush on you is ancient history?" What was *much* more likely was that he was being nice to me so I'd put in a good word with Dina—my pretty, single friend. He must really, *really* like her, too. More than he liked his car, even—and that was saying something for a guy Patrick's age.

"Chocolate," I answered, letting him help me out of the car. My legs were still wobbly. And maybe it was the beginning of a bruise from being thrown against the seat belt in the accident . . . but I kind of doubted it. My chest was aching in an all-too-familiar way. As if my heart was breaking, just a little.

Chapter 14

By the time we finished our milk shakes and drove home, I was too much of a mess to make myself dinner. So even though I discovered that Patrick had carefully arranged the groceries I'd bought on the countertop, with the perishable stuff neatly lined up in the fridge, I ignored them all and had another bland and mushy microwave dinner. Even then, I barely choked it down before talking on the phone with my mom (neglecting, of course, to mention that I'd nearly gotten myself and our neighbor and a guy named Stu killed in a car accident) and falling into bed.

In fact, it wasn't until dinnertime the next day that I really felt much like eating at all, which was a good thing, maybe, since I still didn't have any cereal or bread for breakfast. I had all of Sunday off, so after a day spent reading in bed and getting ahead on chemistry homework, I wandered down to the living room. I was just flipping through the magazines on our coffee table, looking for the crouton recipe that had sparked the whole groceries disaster of the day before, when the phone rang. Obviously, it was my mother. Except for the occasional call from Dina, it always was.

"Elyse!"

"Hi, Mom." I tried to make my voice sound light and bright. "How's it going?"

"Wonderful. You know, Elyse, I like it more here every day." The day before when she'd called, she'd told me about spending the whole afternoon at the hotel spa. "Now I know firsthand what a mustard wrap is!" she'd said proudly. And the day before that, she and Valter had taken some kind of mini cruise. "With a four-course meal!" she'd exclaimed. "They almost had to roll me off the boat."

Today, it seemed, had been just as magical. "As soon as I get home, we're getting your passport renewed," my mother said. "I want to bring you back here for March break next year if we can save up. This morning we went horseback riding down the beach on white stallions, then snorkeling through a barrier reef after lunch. It's four thirty, and I still haven't taken my bathing suit off! I'm just having a drink in my room before an early dinner, then there's a traditional Mexican dance lesson on the beach. How was your day, honey?"

Compared to horseback riding and exploring barrier reefs, boring really. "All right. I stayed home and studied. I'm just about to make dinner."

"Oh. Did you go grocery shopping, then? Did you have to wait long for the bus? I hate to think of you waiting with heavy bags."

"I went yesterday. I was fine," I said, not mentioning that Patrick had actually driven me home. I felt miserable/guilty enough that I wasn't 100 percent happy about his crush on Dina. I didn't need my mother cooing over his wonderfulness again. In the background I heard a door opening, the sound of water running, then an odd whirring noise. "Is housekeeping there?" I asked.

"Oh, no." Was I imagining things, or had my mom just giggled? "That's Valter. They've got full kitchenettes in the rooms with blenders and mini fridges. When they said the resort was five star, they weren't exaggerating. He's just mixing us some frozen cocktails."

Valter was there? In my mother's hotel room? Drinking alcohol? While she had nothing on but that crazy flowered bathing suit with the plunging neckline?

"*Olé*, Elyse!" I heard him call in the background. Well, at least they weren't trying to hide their Mexican love affair from me. Not that that was much of a consolation.

"Listen, sweetie, you know long distance is expensive, so I won't chat for long. I just wanted to remind you about the garbage."

"The garbage?"

"Pickup is first thing tomorrow morning, but you should bring the bins out to the yard tonight so things don't start to smell." I sighed. Right, the garbage. While my mother was off sipping margaritas in a hotel room with a Swedish masseuse, I was on garbage duty. I was about to sigh loudly, but caught myself just in time. After all, this was the first real vacation she'd had since I was born. And, if there *was* something up between her and Valter, it was for sure the first romance she'd had since my dad left. She deserved to have some fun. I just hoped that whatever happened in Mexico would stay in Mexico.

"Sure, Mom. I'll put the garbage out," I promised.

"And how about the house? Any problems?"

"Nope. Everything's fine," I lied. I still hadn't told her about my stupidity with the furnace earlier in the week and, the way I saw it, there was no reason she ever needed to know. "I'm totally on top of things."

"I knew you would be." I heard the unmistakable clinking of glasses.

"I'll let you go, Mom," I said.

"Okay, honey. Love you," she said. "Miss you. I'll call you tomorrow."

"I love you, too," I answered. "Bye."

I set the phone back in the charger and began to shiver, hugging my sweater around me. As interesting as being on my own had been so far, I'd be glad to have my mom back home in a few days. Especially at night, when the wind whipped around the small house, rattling its windowpanes, I felt vulnerable, and more than a little lonely.

To fill up the silence, I turned on some cornball made-for-TV movie. It was called *Pop Star Love* and was about two best friends who were competing for a spot in a rock band, as well as for the love of Zane Steele, the hunky lead singer.

"You betrayed me," one of the girls was shouting. "You don't deserve to win the battle of the bands." Seriously lame stuff, but it provided some background noise. When I finally found the crouton recipe, I went back to the kitchen and started cooking. Between the toasty smell of the warm Parmesan in the kitchen, and the roaring of the crowd at the Battle of the Bands Rock-out Showdown in the living room, it wasn't long before I felt better. I carried my Caesar salad into the living room and ate it with some cold cuts while I watched Cassidy, the underdog-turned-rock-star, win Zane's heart and bring down the house by singing from the heart and expressing her true emotions. I rolled my eyes, then stuffed a giant lettuce leaf into my mouth followed by a homemade crouton. It was warm, crunchy, and just the right amount cheesy. The fancy Parmesan I'd bought had been worth every penny of the $12.75 I'd paid.

When the credits started to roll, I gathered my dishes, brought them to the kitchen, then collected the trash. As instructed by the million-page note my mom had left on the table, I carefully sorted it into different bins—garbage, recyclables, and organic waste—and carried it out to the backyard. When I was done I made some popcorn and wandered back to the TV where Cassidy's tale of romance and rock and roll had been replaced by some creepy crime-scene investigation thing. Great.

A police officer was inching through a darkened house, gun drawn, a look of intense concentration on his face.

The camera cut to a shot of the killer, hiding in a corner of the basement, presumably in the same house. The music faded to an eerie heartbeat, so you just knew that, whatever was coming, it wasn't good. I reached for the remote to change the channel.

Crash. A loud clattering noise came from the back of the house. I jumped, dumping popcorn everywhere, then scrambled onto the couch, tucking my feet up. Instinctively, I hugged a decorative cushion, like its satin trim could somehow protect me. "Oh my God," I said aloud. "Oh my God. Shut up. Shut up. Shut up," I whispered to the TV. I grabbed for the remote a second time and switched the creepy show off. I listened. Silence.

Boom. Another bang from the backyard. I forced myself to take a deep breath. I was just freaked out because of the stupid TV show. It was probably the wind, knocking one of the garbage cans over. Or maybe Patrick or the neighbor on the other side had slammed *their* door and it just sounded like someone was trying to bang their way through mine. There was no reason to panic. Still, just in case, I dropped the useless pillow and reached for the much more practical portable phone. Clutching it tightly, I tiptoed through the spilled popcorn and down the hall toward the kitchen. I had just edged my way carefully around the corner when I heard another loud noise. *Ka-splunk*.

I looked up, then froze. They were unmistakable. Staring at me through the kitchen window over the sink was a set of beady eyes. There was another bang. The door shook. Whoever was outside started to grunt and breathe heavily. They were obviously determined to get in. *Bang*. The door shook again.

Okay, *now* was the time to panic. Practically panting, I ran back to the front of the house. I knew I should have been calling 911, but my hands were shaking so hard, I didn't think I'd be able to dial. Without even stopping to put on boots, I ran out our front door into the snow, over Patrick's conveniently flattened "blossoming Japanese cherry bush" and onto the front porch of his house.

"Help!" I yelled, hammering against the door. "Patrick. It's Elyse. Let me in. Please." I banged at the door again. "Please be home! I need you." A light came on. The door opened slowly.

"Oh, hello," Mr. Connor said, looking up over his reading glasses. Even though it was barely nine P.M., he was dressed in pajama bottoms, a bathrobe, and slippers. "I thought I heard someone knocking. How's the furnace working now, Elyse?" He didn't wait for me to answer. "I don't suppose you've changed your mind about those pickles, have you? I had Patrick bring them up just in case. I'd eat them myself, but they give me indigestion." Just then, Patrick came down the stairs, taking in my panicked expression and sock feet.

I didn't have time to be polite to Mr. Connor, or to explain that I wasn't there to get the stupid pickles. The beady-eyed burglar/murderer could be coming right behind me for all I knew. I pushed my way into the house and turned the deadbolt behind me.

"You have to call the police," I squeaked. "There's somebody in the backyard. They're trying to get into my house. They're banging something against the door, trying to knock it down." Before I knew what was happening, Patrick had come forward and put his arms around me protectively, and I had let him. "I was so scared," I said into his shoulder. "God. And I just took out the garbage, like, two minutes before. Whoever it was was probably watching me. We're wasting time. We have to call the police," I said again. I pulled away from Patrick and tried to dial the portable phone I was still holding. My fingers were shaking badly though, and I'd just managed to press 9 when Patrick took it from me gently.

"You just took out the garbage?" he asked.

I nodded.

"I think I know who it is," he said, putting a hand on my shoulder.

"Who?" He didn't seem at all worried. Like, what? Was it normal in this neighborhood for people to go around trying to break down other people's doors? He made rings with his hands and held them up over his eyes like binoculars. Was he suggesting some rogue bird-watchers were on the loose? I seriously didn't have time to play charades.

"Raccoons," he explained finally. His grandfather nodded behind him.

"Coons are bad this time of year," the old man

concurred. "They've been holed up most of the winter, but now it's mating season. They get hungry. If you put your garbage out without a coon-proof strap, they'll get it. No question."

"But I don't think you understand," I said, reaching for the phone again. "Whoever it was, they were *right* at the door—banging on it. I saw their eyes."

"They've got coon-proof straps down at Winner's Hardware for five ninety-nine," Patrick's grandfather went on, like he hadn't heard me. "Up near the cash register. But if you can't find them, the guy you want to ask is Johnny."

"But the person was breathing. Heavy breathing," I said loudly, enunciating my words. "And grunting, too. The whole door was shaking." I made a shaking motion with my hands. "On its hinges."

"Oh, yes. Coons'll do that." The old man nodded again. "You get 'em hungry enough, the coons around here will definitely do that." He took his glasses off, tucking them into the pocket of his robe. "Well, that's it for me. Good night, young lady. Patrick, see you in the morning." He started to shuffle up the stairs, like there was nothing else to say. Halfway up, he turned. "So you're sure you won't be needing those pickles, then?" he asked.

"No," I answered. "No pickles. Thanks."

"Righty-oh, then. Patrick, see that Elyse here gets home safely, will you?" Patrick nodded.

"Patrick," I said urgently, as soon as his grandfather had

turned again. "You've *got* to believe me. This was no raccoon." I grabbed hold of his arms, squeezing so hard I probably cut off his circulation. I couldn't seem to make myself let go though.

"Okay. I believe you." He squeezed my other arm gently in return. "I'll go check it out. Don't worry." He put his boots on. "You stay here."

"No way," I said. "I'm coming with you. What if the guy's still there? What if he's armed? Or crazy? Or armed *and* crazy? You should have seen his eyes. They were wild."

"All the more reason you should stay here," he said, shrugging on his coat.

If I was being honest, I *really* didn't want to go anywhere near whoever—or whatever—had been trying to break through my back door, but I couldn't let Patrick face it alone, either. I'd never be able to live with myself if something happened to him.

"I've got the phone," I said, holding it up. "I can call 911 if you need me to."

"Okay," he answered, "as long as you stay at the side of the house." I nodded, agreeing to the compromise. "But you need a coat. And shoes." My snow-covered socks were starting to leave puddles on the front hall tiles, and—I hadn't noticed until that second—my feet were beginning to burn from the cold. He pulled a blue jacket and a pair of old Nikes out of the closet and I slid them on. The coat sleeves hung way down over my hands, and the shoes were about nine sizes too big. The first step I took, I nearly tripped over the toes and fell into the banister. Patrick extended his arm and I took it to steady myself.

"You ready?" he asked. I nodded. He grabbed a flashlight from the closet and we headed out the door.

When we reached the laneway between our houses he motioned for me to stop. I pressed my back against the wall of my house, my heart pounding, as I watched him open the gate. "Be careful," I whispered. For a few seconds, I could hear the squeak of his boots against the snow. Then nothing.

A truck rumbled past. A dog barked. I scrunched my hands up inside Patrick's blue jacket and flipped the collar up around my face to keep from shivering. It smelled comforting and familiar. I inhaled again. Like Patrick: coffee and sawdust and engine grease.

A minute passed. Then two. "Patrick?" I whispered loudly. No answer. "Patrick?" Working up my courage, I took a step toward the backyard. I could hear the grunting noise again, and the heavy breathing. "Patrick?" I whispered even more loudly. Something was wrong. I just knew it. I pulled my hand out of the coat sleeve and punched in the first two numbers: 9-1. Then, with my finger poised over the 1, I slowly opened the back gate. "Patrick?" I said again.

I took two more steps. *Crash.* A metallic banging noise filled the air. "Hyaaaaaa!" someone shouted, ninja style. I jumped straight up, dropping the phone into the snow, and instinctively raised my arms over my face to take cover. A second later, I looked up. There was Patrick, standing in the middle of my yard, holding two old garbage can lids like cymbals.

He smiled when he saw me. "Don't worry. I scared them away," he said proudly.

"Them?" I looked around frantically, just in time to catch sight of two bushy tails disappearing into a gap underneath the hedge.

"Yeah. It was raccoons all right. They got your trash." I followed his gaze. Garbage was strewn across the deck and all over the yard. The organic waste bin was propped against the door at an odd angle, its contents emptied.

I was still barely able to breathe. "You don't think you could have warned me before you did that?" I pointed at the garbage can lids.

The proud look fell from his face. "Did I scare you?"

My heart was beating so fast I thought I might faint. "Yeah. You could say that." I dropped to my knees and started to dig through the snow for the phone, glad for the excuse not to have to look him in the eye. Even in the cold, my cheeks were burning with embarrassment. Obviously it had only been raccoons. If I'd just opened the back door, I would have seen that for myself. I was such a coward; such an idiot for running into Patrick's arms like a scared little girl. First the furnace, then the groceries, and now this. Here I'd thought I was so smart and so independent . . . then the second my mom went away, I'd gone straight to some guy for help. Some guy I barely knew.

Some guy who was only being so nice to me because he was in love with my best friend.

A second later, Patrick was down on his knees beside me, helping to dig. He found the phone, pulled it out, and pressed the talk button. Even from where I was sitting, two feet away, I could tell there was no dial tone.

"Oh man," he said. "Sorry. It's busted." He pressed the talk button a few more times to be sure, then examined the handset carefully. "I can try to fix it if you want. I'm pretty sure my grandpa has a screwdriver that will open it. I got a B+ in electronics class."

"No," I said, taking it from him. "It's okay. I can do it." Except that I knew I couldn't. I didn't know the first thing about fixing a phone.

"Well, at least let me help you pick up this garbage, then."

"No, really." I pushed myself to my feet, brushing snow off my knees. There were tears in my eyes, and I didn't want him to see. "I'll do it. It's my garbage." My stupid mistake, I thought, my responsibility. "You don't always have to help me." I picked a soup can out of the snow and tossed it back into the recycling bin, then reached down for a mayonnaise jar. "And you don't always have to be so nice to me."

"I kind of like helping you," he said, digging his hands into his pockets as he watched me work. "And being nice to you. We're friends, right?"

"Yeah, sure, we're friends. But you haven't even

known me that long. I'm just some girl who moved in next door." I gathered two flattened cereal boxes and an egg carton. "Seriously, I can clean this up by myself. It's not your responsibility. None of it is. Don't worry about it."

"You're crying," he said suddenly. "What's wrong?"

What *was* wrong? How could I explain it to him when I barely understood it myself? I was embarrassed, and sad, and so *so* angry. Behind the jokes I made and the tough front I put up, I felt scared and alone a lot of the time—but now more than ever. At a time when I needed friends the most, I couldn't seem to let anybody in.

What was wrong was that the last time I'd opened up my heart and admitted to needing somebody, he'd turned around and flattened it to a pulp. What was wrong was that my new best friend, who deserved all the happiness in the world, was about to get it, and it was making me miserable. What was wrong, I realized fully with a shock, was that I had fallen completely and utterly in love . . . again . . . with someone who didn't love me back . . . and I was terrified. More terrified than I'd ever been in my life.

I looked at Patrick. His eyes were wide with worry.

"Nothing's wrong," I said, ducking down for more garbage. "I just . . . scratched my hand on a can lid. That's all."

"Do you want me to take a look?" he said, coming toward me. "I can get you a Band-Aid or something."

"No," I snapped. I couldn't stand another minute of his niceness. I didn't want his Band-Aids. I couldn't accept his outstretched hand. If I leaned on him, he'd only let me down eventually, anyway. Falling in love was just the first step toward getting your heart broken. I knew that. And not only that, if I did admit to Patrick that I was falling for him, and he *did* like me back, it would mean betraying my only real friend. Dina deserved better than that. So much better. Sure, Patrick had had a crush on me before, but it was ancient history now. He wanted to be with Dina, and she wanted to be with him. Which left me alone, exactly how I'd said I wanted to be.

"Go inside, Patrick. I don't want your help." I grabbed the snow shovel and started piling the organic waste back into the bin. Patrick just stood there. "I said go inside. I can do this on my own. Just leave me alone. Just don't come near me."

"Sure," he said. I could see him biting his lip in confusion. He backed away slowly, giving me my space—like I was some kind of frightened animal. "Okay, Elyse. Good night."

I didn't answer. Instead I slammed the lid of the organic waste bin shut, accidentally pinching my finger. I yelped, then threw the shovel down in the snow in frustration. With tears still streaming down my face, I marched up the steps and into my empty house.

Chapter 15

The second I'd slammed the door behind me, I covered my face and crumpled into a ball on the kitchen floor, letting my tears soak the sleeves of Patrick's blue jacket. A few minutes later, when the sobs had worked their way out of my body, I kicked off the pair of too-big Nikes he'd loaned me. My socks were wet and my feet were freezing, but I didn't care. I deserved it. I'd acted like such an idiot.

Patrick must have thought I was insane. He'd only been trying to help me and I'd thrown it back in his face. And the worst part was I'd have to see him the next day for our driving lesson, *and* at work, *and* around the house. I sniffed and wiped at my eyes, trying to calm myself down. Maybe it wasn't the end of the world. He was a really nice guy, right? I'd just have to apologize to him somehow and explain (without revealing Dina's crush or my feelings for him) why I'd behaved like the world's biggest jerk. After all, a guy who bought you a milk shake after you'd just almost crashed his car wasn't the type to hold a grudge.

And even if—worst case scenario—he never wanted to

be my friend again, at the very least I had to smooth things over enough that we could be civil to each other, especially since he was going to end up dating Dina. I couldn't afford to lose her, too.

I had just pushed myself to my feet when I heard another loud banging noise. Then more snuffling and grunting. The raccoons were back but I wasn't scared this time. I flung the door open. "Go!" I shouted at one who was halfway down the porch steps, dragging an empty cookie package behind it. It sat up on its fat haunches, looking at me quizzically before going right back to its chocolate chip cookie crumbs. "Shoo!" I yelled, waving my arms. The second one popped its head out of the organic waste bin to see what was going on, decided I was unworthy of its attention, and returned to gnawing on some gross, old pork chop scraps. "Okay, fine then." I threw up my hands. "Enjoy your meal." I slammed the door again. I'd just get up early to clean the mess again before the garbage trucks arrived. I didn't have the energy to stand guard all night anyway, plus, they clearly weren't afraid of me.

But the next morning, when I dragged myself out of bed in time to do the cleanup and get the garbage bins to the curb, the yard was spotless. In fact, if it wasn't for the big indents the tipped bins had made in the snow and the faint trail of cookie crumbs leading down the steps, I almost might have been able to convince myself that the whole thing had never happened.

Had the garbage fairy paid a visit overnight? Somehow,

I doubted it. There was only one possible explanation for this good deed. I leaned out the door to get a view of Patrick's house, but nobody was in the yard and the curtains were all closed. Hugging my bathrobe around me, I walked to the front of the house and peered out. There were our bins, neatly arranged at the end of our driveway—our *perfectly shoveled* driveway. How early must Patrick have had to wake up to do all of this in secret? And why had he bothered after I'd been so mean to him?

Well, I'd have the chance to ask him when I apologized that afternoon before our driving lesson. Until then, there wasn't much I could do. I had to get ready for school.

All day long, I tried my best to focus on kinetic molecular theory and logarithmic functions, but my mind kept wandering back to Patrick . . . his crinkly eyed smile and curly hair, his unending kindness, and his incredible optimism in the face of my horrible driving skills. But, most of all, the shocked, confused expression on his face when I'd told him I didn't want his help the night before. I didn't know what, exactly, I'd say to him. Still, I found myself counting down the hours until I could see him again and set things right.

"Are you okay?" Dina asked finally as she drove us to the mall for work that afternoon. I knew I'd been quiet and distant all day at school, but there was no way to tell her what had happened without revealing my feelings for Patrick.

"Yeah. Sure," I lied. "I just miss my mom, I guess. And

maybe I'm nervous about my driving test."

"I'm not surprised," Dina said. "You and your mom are really close, right? She'll be home soon, though. And, seriously, if what Patrick tells me is true, you really don't have to worry about passing your road test tomorrow. He says you're an awesome driver."

"You were talking to him?" I asked. "Today? Did he call you?" I could hear the desperation in my own voice and silently prayed that Dina wouldn't pick up on it.

"Oh. No," she said. "I haven't talked to him since he was in the store yesterday. Did you know that he bought enough cards to get a Cupid doll? Who do you think he's going to give it to?"

"I don't know for sure," I answered, looking at her meaningfully, "but I have a pretty good idea."

A wide smile broke across her face just as her phone started to buzz. We pulled into a parking space and she reached down, taking it out of her bag. "Seriously," she said with an exaggerated sigh when I looked at her questioningly, hoping it was Patrick. She flipped the phone shut. "My mom just keeps texting me all day long. I'm losing my mind." But she didn't look like she was losing her mind. If anything, she looked positively content. I guessed that when the guy you'd been crushing on liked you back enough to give you a tacky, singing doll, it tended to put things like an overbearing mother into perspective.

The time passed slowly at work that day. But when

quarter to six finally came around, I stationed myself in the pen aisle to wait. We had a new shipment of liquid ultra gels in, and I'd already tested them out. They were crisp *and* smooth *and* rolly, without a hint of sploodgy-ness. If that didn't make Patrick forgive me, I figured nothing would. But six fifteen came and went, and there was no sign of him.

"Did Patrick call?" I asked Dina, who was busy tex-ting on her cell. "Can you check if there are any messages?" There weren't.

I hung around the store another fifteen minutes, then made my way to the key-cutting kiosk. Maybe he'd just lost track of time.

A big, burly guy with a tattoo of a killer whale on his arm was busy working the key-cutting machine. I had to repeat myself three times before he could hear me over the high-pitched grinding noise. "I'm looking for Patrick."

"Huh?"

"Patrick."

"Who?"

"PATRICK."

He shut the machine off, and handed a gleaming gold key to a woman wearing a leather jacket.

"Oh," he said as he made change for the woman. "You must be Elyse." I looked at him in surprise. "Sorry. I was supposed to come find you, but it's been so busy I haven't had a chance. Patrick wanted me to give you this." He reached underneath the counter and pulled out a box. On the side was a photo of a cordless phone with two handsets. It looked all sleek and space-aged and seemed to have about ten million features. There was no way it could have been cheap.

"I can't take that," I said immediately.

"Yeah. He said you'd say that," answered the guy. Then he held out his hand. "I'm Jax, by the way."

"Nice to meet you." I shook his hand. "I'm Elyse. But, then, you knew that."

He pulled a folded piece of paper out of his pocket and started to read from it. "Okay. He said to tell you the phone was on sale, and so he can't return it. Plus, anyway, he already lost the receipt." I sighed. "He also says he has to cancel your driving lessons because he's got scurvy. He'll probably be sick all week, at least, but he says not to worry, you don't need him anymore anyway. Because you're an awesome driver."

"Give me that," I said, taking the paper from Jax. Written in point form, in smooth black ink, were more or less the exact things Jax had just told me—with one exception. At the very bottom, underlined three times, was the word "Sorry."

"Did he say anything else?" I asked, although I didn't know what I was hoping for, exactly.

"Nah," Jax replied. "But, between you and me, he's lying about the scurvy. He's just avoiding you."

Well, that much, at least, was kind of obvious.

"Thanks," I said, picking up the phone and tucking it

under my arm. "If you do see him, could you tell him—"

"Uh-uh. Sorry," Jax interrupted me. He pointed to the sign in front of him. THE KEYHOLE. "I cut keys. I don't take messages." I nodded. "Don't take it personal, or anything. I just know better than to get involved in a lovers' quarrel."

"Right. Thanks anyway." I turned and left. He obviously couldn't help me, so there wasn't any point explaining to him that, for it to be a lovers' quarrel, you'd need *two* people to be in love.

It felt weird to take the bus by myself, and weirder even to come home and walk past Patrick's house. The red car was parked in the driveway, so I knew he was home, but the curtains were still closed tightly.

I threw my bag on the front steps, setting the cordless phone beside it, and walked back to the end of the driveway to collect the garbage bins. And that was when I noticed them: black nylon straps, bolted to the tops of each bin with buckles that opened and closed. Tiny pictures of raccoons ran along their length. The Patrick fairy had struck again.

Later that night, when I went down to the basement to do a desperately needed load of laundry, I discovered one more good deed: the huge, heavy wardrobe that had tipped on top of my mother was standing upright, pushed against the wall. Patrick had returned my key days ago. So obviously he'd done this when he'd been in to put away the groceries. But how? My mom and I combined couldn't lift that thing. And then I remembered Patrick had been on his way to pick up Jax that day. He must have roped Jax into helping him with the wardrobe, since it was clear his friend and coworker didn't share his annoyingly overly helpful nature.

I opened and closed the wardrobe door, noticing how the cracked wood had been glued back together, then sighed again. Knowing that Patrick was falling in love with Dina, and especially after the way I'd treated him, every nice thing he did felt like a tiny knife going through my heart. Why wouldn't he just stop already?

But he didn't stop. The next morning, the driveway had been magically shoveled again, and a thin layer of Patrick's trademark salt had been spread over the icy patches. For someone who lived next door and worked at the same mall, he also continued to avoid me in a truly spectacular way. Twice, I snuck out while Dina covered the cash, hoping to see him at the Keyhole, but both times Jax told me I'd just missed him.

Dina swore she hadn't seen or heard from him either. "Oh no. I hope he's not sick again," she worried. "Do you think he'll still show up for the panda party?" Considering the way he felt about her, I thought it was a safe bet that even his fake scurvy wouldn't keep him away and—when he showed up to see Dina—I intended to be there to talk to him. We couldn't go on like this forever, after all. He'd have to face me on Valentine's Day. I could wait.

Or, at least, I thought I could wait . . . until that

Thursday, after another day Patrick had spent avoiding me. I was just finishing my shift and starting to cash out when I heard a familiar voice. "Elyse." I looked up. "I was on my way home from the hospital, and I just had to come in and say thank you." My favorite customer, Mrs. Conchetti, was standing near the counter with tears in her eyes. "Little Nolan made it through his heart surgery. The doctors are saying he's going to be just fine."

"Oh, Mrs. Conchetti. That's such a relief." I actually came around the counter and hugged her. It wasn't something I'd do with any other customer, but over the past few months I'd gotten to know her and I'd heard so much about her family. The occasion just seemed to call for it.

"We'd just heard the good news from the doctor when that curly-haired delivery boy of yours arrived. And I have to tell you, your thoughtfulness meant the world to me. And to my son and daughter-in-law."

My curly-haired delivery boy?

"The second I saw the Cupid doll, I knew it was from you. We put it right beside Nolan's crib, so he saw it as soon as he woke up. He's still so weak, the poor thing. But I think he almost smiled when it started to sing." Mrs. Conchetti grabbed hold of me again, squeezing me tightly against her ample chest. Then she pulled away before giving me two smacking Italian-style kisses—one on each cheek. "You're a beautiful girl," she told me. "Beautiful inside and out."

Before I had a chance to correct her, or to ask her

what she was talking about, she glanced at her watch. "I should go. My son and daughter-in-law are spending the night at the hospital. I told them I'd bring dinner. You can't eat anything they serve in the cafeteria there. It all tastes like glue." She actually pinched my cheek. "Thank you," she said again, and then she was gone.

I dropped the coins I'd been counting back into the cash and sat down, trying to put the pieces together. A curly-haired delivery boy? A Cupid doll? I remembered how Patrick had been standing beside the counter when Mrs. Conchetti had come in to tell me the news about the baby. . . . How I'd said I wished there was something I could do. . . . How Patrick had immediately bought eleven valentines with all the money he had, getting his customer loyalty card stamped, then coming back for four more the next day. Fifteen in all—but they *weren't* for fifteen girls. That much was clear now. It was all making sense . . . except that it also wasn't.

Up until the last few days, it had seemed like all the nice things Patrick was doing were designed to impress Dina. But bringing the Cupid doll to the hospital? Shoveling my driveway? The raccoon-proof straps? Why was Patrick being so nice to me?

I'd been wrong about him. The Cupid doll had made that much clear. He wasn't a player and he wasn't a pig. He was sweet, caring, and genuine—the elusive two percent. So different from Matt Love that the two barely belonged in the same category of humankind. But then again, Patrick could have been a full-fledged and official saint and it wouldn't have mattered. I'd already told him I didn't date. Also, he'd made it crystal clear that his crush on me was history, and that he was interested in Dina.

Which just brought me right back to my original question: Why was he being so nice to me? Did he still think it might somehow help him to score points with Dina? Or, if that wasn't it, did he have some kind of rare disorder? (Not scurvy, obviously, but some genetic brain disease that led to chronic niceness?) Or was he just trying to drive me crazy with guilt for having been so mean to him?

Whatever the explanation was, this couldn't go on. I needed to find out what was up, and I couldn't wait until Valentine's Day to do it, either.

Chapter 16

The first thing I did when I got home from work that day was march into the kitchen to find the jacket Patrick had let me borrow on the night of the raccoons. I also picked up the too-big Nikes, sliding them into a plastic bag. Then I had a handful of crackers with cheese. (It was bad enough having to confront Patrick without doing it on an empty stomach.) Then I went upstairs to make sure there weren't any cheese bits stuck between my teeth and to put on some lip gloss. Then I tied my hair back into a ponytail and looked at myself from different angles in the mirror. Then I decided the ponytail made my face look too pointy, took out the elastic, and let my hair down. Then I checked my teeth again, just to be certain.

But then . . . *then* I marched right out the front door like a girl on a mission. I was halfway down the front path, stomping through the snow, when I remembered I'd forgotten something: the opal pendant. Each day, since the afternoon I'd discovered it belonged to Patrick's grandmother, I'd been making myself mental notes to return it. And, each day, for one reason or another, I'd convinced myself it wasn't quite the right time. The night I'd shouted at Patrick in the backyard, I'd carefully placed it in a small wooden box I kept in my desk drawer, coiling the chain carefully before closing the lid. Now I ran back up the stairs in my boots, tracking snow across the hardwood to retrieve it.

A minute later, I was back on Patrick's doorstep. Taking a deep breath, I grabbed the knocker and banged it three times. The red car, still in the driveway, was covered by a thin layer of snow. Patrick *had* to be home. I knocked again. The sound echoed across the empty street, and still nobody answered. I walked back up the path and looked at the upstairs windows, expecting to see the flick of a curtain closing. I knew Patrick was inside, but he was determined to avoid me. Well, too bad, I thought. I picked up the knocker again. I'd stay there all night if I needed to. I'd knock until all the other neighbors complained about the noise. I'd bang on that door until my fingers went numb and my nose started to run from the cold and the snow piled up all around me. I'd knock until the sun—

"Oh. Elyse. Good to see you again." The door opened and Patrick's grandfather peered out. "You've come back for the pickles." He smiled and slid his reading glasses into his pocket, motioning for me to come in. "They've got a good crunch to them. You won't be disappointed." I stomped the snow off my boots and stepped into the house. Then I wiped the fog off my glasses and put them back on, looking around for signs of Patrick.

"Oh, no. I'm sure they're really crunchy," I said as patiently as I could manage. "But I just came to talk to Patrick about something." My heart was beating fast and my palms were sweaty—just being in his house—just wondering how on earth I was going to begin this impossible conversation.

"Well now." The old man glanced at his watch. "Patrick's gone out with a friend to practice his music. I don't expect him back anytime soon."

"But isn't that his car out front?" I didn't mean for the words to come out in the accusing tone that they did, but if Patrick was hiding upstairs—if his grandfather was lying to me—I had to find out.

Mr. Connor went to the front window and looked out into the driveway. "That it is," he said, nodding. "He must have walked. Jax doesn't live very far from here."

"Oh." I gulped, feeling like a jerk yet again. What kind of person accuses a sweet old man of lying to her face? A person like me, apparently. "Right. I'll get going then. Sorry to have disturbed you."

"Quite all right," Mr. Connor said, shuffling toward the kitchen. "You haven't disturbed me at all. Actually, I'm glad you came by. I was just about to put the kettle on. Would you stay for a cup of tea?"

"Oh, no. Really. Thanks. I should go."

"Wonderful," Mr. Connor said, "Earl Grey or orange pekoe?" Clearly he didn't have his hearing aid in, again. "Now, I hope you don't take honey, because I'm afraid we're all out. But I keep a bag of butter cookies hidden in the vegetable crisper where Patrick won't see them. He's always worrying about my cholesterol, but I only have one every now and then."

"I—" I started, meaning to make my excuses in a much louder voice, but then I stopped myself. After all, what was the harm in having a cup of tea with Patrick's grandfather? It wasn't like I had anything important to do at home by myself, except for obsessing over how nervous I was about my driving test the next day, and how anxious I was about what I was going to say to Patrick when I finally did track him down. "I love butter cookies," I finished, instead. "And Earl Grey is great, if you've got it." I took off my boots, hung up Patrick's coat in the closet, and dumped the bag with the Nikes near the stairs before following Mr. Connor into the kitchen.

A few minutes later, over a steaming cup of Earl Grey, Mr. Connor cleared his throat. "Now," he said, sliding the plate of cold, store-bought butter cookies toward me and lowering himself carefully onto a kitchen chair, "Elyse. I'm sure *you* can tell me. What is a subwoofer?"

"Umm . . ." I stalled, caught by surprise. I'd been figuring we might talk about the weather, or else swap stories about people we knew who had diseases. Wasn't that what old people liked to do?

"It sounds like something to do with a submarine, or something about a dog," Patrick's grandfather went on, "but that can't be right."

"It's a music thing," I said. "A kind of speaker, I think."

He slapped the table. "That would be it. The names young people think up these days." He shook his head. "Subwoofer. That's what Patrick and Jax were working on. For a get-together. Testing the subwoofer. It's got something to do with a little song he's been rehearsing, about a girl with brown eyes." I gulped and sat up straighter. His song was about Dina—Dina and her big brown eyes. I tried not to let the pain I was feeling show on my face. "You see, he thinks I've always got my hearing aid switched off." The old man pulled on one earlobe. "But I don't miss much."

"Mr. Connor?" I asked, leaning forward. I had to find out what was going on.

"Oh. Frank. Call me Frank."

"Okay. Frank?" I felt weird saying it. "Can I ask you something? Is Patrick nice to everyone?"

"Well. I suppose. . . ."

"I don't mean just nice. But, you know, really nice? Over-the-top nice? He shoveled my driveway twice this week. And he bought me those raccoon-proof straps, plus a new phone even though it was my fault the old phone broke in the first place. And that's barely the beginning of the list. There were the free driving lessons, and he baked me cookies, and brought my groceries home, plus he fixed my furnace and our broken wardrobe."

"Well. If he's been doing all that, that would explain it," Frank said.

"Explain what?"

"Why he's been singing in the shower the last few weeks. Patrick's like his grandmother. My late wife, Jeannie. You've never seen anyone who got a kick out of helping others the way she did. Buy her jewelry or take her out to a fancy restaurant and she'd thank you kindly, but give her a bake sale to plan, a Girl Scout troop to lead, or a stray cat to nurse back to health and then you'd see her in her element. Her face would light up. Her whole outlook would change. But then, that's all of us in some ways, I suppose," he said philosophically, blowing on his tea to cool it. "Everyone needs to be needed. Even an old man like me."

I squeezed my mug, letting the warmth seep into my fingers. *Everyone needs to be needed.* I'd never thought about it quite that way before.

"Now, take Patrick for example," Frank went on. "When my wife died, I lost my rudder for a while there. Who wouldn't, after fifty-five years of marriage? But I've got some get-up-and-go in me yet. I could shovel the driveway and get my own meals. I do, sometimes, but other times, I let Patrick look after me. Do you know why?" he asked. I was pretty sure I knew the answer, but I let him go on. "First of all, because I like the company. You get old like me, you don't want to be alone watching *Jeopardy!* all day. For one thing, you start to see repeats, so you know all the answers, but that's not the worst of it. The worst of it is the quiet in the house. Just the length of the days. But I also like having Patrick here because Patrick likes to be here. There's something to be said for doing everything yourself—being independent. Losing that independence is the hardest thing about old age—but then again, sometimes the greatest gift you can give someone else is to accept whatever it is they've got to offer you." He reached for a butter cookie and bit in, letting the crumbs fall to his plate. "Some of his music is dreadful and loud, mind you," he added. "Even when I haven't got my hearing aid in. But that's a small price to pay."

I reached for another cookie, wondering what to make of all that. So, Patrick liked helping people. But what did that make me? Just some desperate, helpless, driving-impaired charity case he'd decided to take on? Because if *that* was what he thought of me, I didn't care if I ever saw him again.

"He's just like Jeannie. It's uncanny, really. I don't think I ever saw my wife so happy as the time, early on in our marriage, when I fell off the roof and broke both my legs." Patrick's grandfather actually laughed at the memory. "For once, I had no choice but to let her wait on me hand and foot. But I got better at letting her do things for me as the years went on. You see those pictures over there?" He pointed at the far wall where three small landscapes were hanging, side by side. One was a painting of a lake. Another was a tree in front of a sunset, and the third was a field with a windmill in it.

"Jeannie picked those out in a gift shop one time when we traveled out west. Gave them to me for my birthday.

Do you notice anything about them?"

I stood up and walked toward the paintings. They were each in a heavy gold-edged frame but, besides that, there was nothing especially remarkable about them. It was the kind of art you usually saw in badly decorated waiting rooms, or old peoples' houses. In fact, I could remember my grandmother having some practically identical paintings in her hallway.

"They're really nice," I lied, not wanting to hurt Mr. Connor's feelings.

"They are, aren't they? But they're crooked. That's what I can't help but see. Jeannie hung them up herself. I was a cabinetmaker before I retired, so I know about making things level. But she bought me those and snuck them home in her suitcase. She hung them up the night before my birthday to surprise me, and she was so proud of herself, I've never had the heart to straighten them. So they've just stayed there. For, oh, I don't know. The last fifteen years. Crooked."

He looked fondly at the cheesy, misaligned landscapes and I followed his gaze. Now that he mentioned it, I could see it clearly. The one on the left-hand side was almost a full inch higher up on the wall than the other two. And the middle one tilted slightly to the right. You'd have to really love somebody, I thought, to put up with fifteen years of pretending you didn't notice something like that.

Which reminded me . . . I slid a hand into my pocket and pulled out the pendant, putting it on the table in front of him. I sat down again. "I almost forgot. I found this," I said. "I've been meaning to bring it over." He took the necklace and laid the pendant in the palm of his hand. "I thought it might be yours. Or, I mean, Jeannie's."

"Well. I'll be." Patrick's grandfather squinted at it more closely.

"There's an inscription on the back," I said, in case he'd forgotten or the writing would be too small for him to see. "It says, 'MBW took AC 23-03-1917.'"

"Where did you find this?" he asked.

"Our attic. My mom found it between some floorboards, and then the first time I was over here, I noticed your wife was wearing one just like it in your wedding photo."

"MBW. Mabel Beth Wain. That was my mother. And AC. Arthur Connor. My father."

So that explained the dates. It belonged to Patrick's *great*-grandmother. It *really was* nearly a hundred years old.

"My father gave this to my mother on the occasion of their engagement. When she took him to be her husband. Jeannie wore it on our wedding day. I'm sure you've heard of the tradition. What is it now? Something gold, something blue . . ."

"Something old, something new, something borrowed, and something blue." I helped him out. I'd watched enough romantic comedies with my mother to know.

"That's it. This was three of the four. Old, blue, and borrowed. She was supposed to give it back to my mother after the wedding, but she lost it. Jeannie felt just awful about that, I remember."

"How do you think it got into our attic?"

"We were married in that house. Did Patrick tell you that?" I shook my head. "My father built it, and Jeannie and I lived there until my parents died, at which time we sold it and moved back to the old house. We had our wedding service right out there, in the backyard, under the blossoming Japanese cherry tree."

So there *was* a blossoming Japanese cherry. But it was a tree, not a shrub, and it was in our backyard, not Patrick's front garden. And I *hadn't* crushed it into a pile of twigs with the car!

I glanced over at Mr. Connor as he gently twirled the chain around his pockmarked hand. I pictured Patrick's grandmother Jeannie in her lace wedding gown, descending our staircase to meet him, reaching out for his hand to steady herself in her high heels. I saw Mr. Connor looking at her, the way he was looking at the pendant now—with tender, bleary eyes—as they were about to embark on a lifetime together.

"Thank you," he said, closing his hand around it. "I didn't imagine I'd ever see this again."

"No," I said, putting my cup in the sink and clearing away both our cookie plates. "Thank you." Although, I wasn't exactly sure what I was thanking him for . . . the tea maybe, or the cookies, or just for spending the time, sitting there talking with me. "I should get going," I said, glancing at the old-fashioned clock on the wall. "I have my driving test tomorrow. When Patrick gets home, could you tell him I was here?" I asked.

"Absolutely, I'll do that," Frank said, pushing himself up from his chair. "I'm not good for much these days, but I can pass along a message." And that was when I noticed the jar, sitting in the corner beside the refrigerator.

"Hey," I said anxiously. "Would it be all right if I changed my mind . . . about those pickles?"

Mr. Connor's face lit up. And I don't think it was my imagination: He stood just a little taller. "I think that would be just fine," he answered. I walked over and picked up the jar. It must have weighed twenty pounds. What the hell was I going to do with twenty pounds of dill pickles? "If you slice those, you can put them on a roast beef sandwich," Patrick's grandfather said, as if reading my mind. "Or you can chop them up. Put them in a tuna salad. Jeannie used to do that."

"Mmmmm," I said. "Thanks. Thanks a lot." I hugged the enormous jar to my chest. Pickles and tuna? It sounded disgusting. But then again, it barely mattered. I stepped out into the snow with Mr. Connor's words echoing in my head: *Sometimes the greatest gift you can give someone is to accept whatever it is they've got to offer you.*

I knew now exactly what I needed to do to make things right.

Chapter 17

I spent that evening covered in a fine dust of flour and icing sugar. I started with the pinwheel cookies, rolling the dough into a log and putting it in the fridge to chill, then moved on to the black-and-white cheesecake. Once I had it in the oven, I was ready to tackle my new, top secret project. I just got the layers baked before I collapsed into bed, waking early the next morning to do the decorating. Thankfully, I'd taken the entire day off work and school for my driving test, which was that afternoon.

By the time I was done icing and packing everything into Tupperware containers, I was exhausted again but, in a way, it was a good thing. My baking frenzy successfully kept my mind off the test, not to mention the fact that it was Valentine's Day—exactly one year to the day I'd had my heart broken into a million pieces. In fact, I barely had time to think about either one of those things until my mom called me from the poolside guest services phone to remind me my aunt Sarah would be there to pick me up for my road test at one thirty—like I could have forgotten.

"You ready, sweetie?" she asked. Somewhere in the background, a live band was playing a bad cover of Elvis Presley's "Can't Help Falling in Love." The lead singer had a thick, Spanish accent.

"Sure," I sighed. "Why not?" I was as ready as I'd ever be.

And it turned out I wasn't even lying. In a way, I thought—while I sat outside Dina's house that night in the car, working up the nerve to go in—things had come full circle. Here it was, Valentine's Day again. And I was about to get my heart broken, again. Dina and Patrick liked each other. I was certain. Tonight would be the night he'd tell her, through song. And I had stupidly let myself fall for Patrick. So, yet again, I was about to lose the guy I loved to my best friend. But there was a difference this time, and it was a big one. This time, I was losing him to somebody who truly deserved him. I turned the keys, pulling them out of the ignition with a small sniff.

Plus, I hadn't come out of the experience empty-handed. Thanks to Patrick, I was a licensed driver. With the exception of saying I'd parked an "eensy bit too close to the curb," the examiner had given me a perfect score.

That hadn't changed the fact that I was a nervous wreck driving by myself for the first time, of course, or the fact that it turned out I had zero sense of direction. By the time I actually managed to find Dina's place—which I'd been to a bunch of times on the bus before—it was 8:30. The party had started over an hour ago. I headed up the walkway, carrying my cardboard box of stuffed pandas with Tupperware containers of black and white snacks balanced precariously on top. I could hear the bass from the music vibrating through the walls. Patrick and Jax had obviously done a good job with the subwoofer.

The door was slightly ajar and I pushed it open with my foot. For a party dedicated to a cuddly endangered species, I was surprised to be able to report: What I found inside was decidedly un-lame. Guys and girls (most of whom I recognized from school) were clustered in groups—the guys looking more put-together than usual, all dressed in black, while the girls were in different, cute, black and white outfits. I suddenly felt way too casual in my plain black pants (usually part of my Goodman's Gifts & Stationery uniform) and tight white T-shirt. The living room—where most people seemed to be—was decorated with black and white helium balloons and white streamers that looked kind of cool and sophisticated with the lights turned down low.

The music was loud and a few kids were busy playing pin the tail on the panda in the dining room. They were spinning a blindfolded girl around so fast I was afraid for the safety of Dina's parents' good china, but everyone was laughing, including the girl.

I couldn't see Patrick anywhere, but I recognized a

girl from my chemistry class, Erin. "Hey," I said, trying to peer around my stack of boxes and Tupperware. "Do you know where Dina is?"

"Sorry," she said. "I just got here. Haven't seen her."

"She's in the kitchen," said a guy's voice from the other side of me. I adjusted my snack foods, trying to see who it was—and when I did manage to get a view around the Tupperware, I nearly dropped ten hours worth of baking. His shoulders were broader than when I'd met him at Christmas break. His face had more stubble, but he had that same dopey, clueless grin.

"Damien? What are you doing here?"

"Good to see you again, too." He laughed. Okay, obviously, he'd caught me by surprise. I hadn't managed to hide the disdain in my voice. But what did he want me to do after he'd broken my best friend's heart before running off to the College of Babes and Beer? Hug him?

"Here, give me that." He took the cheesecake and two other Tupperware containers, leaving me with the box of stuffed animals. "Come on," he said, clearing a path through the people gathered in the hallway and leading the way to the kitchen.

"Hey, babe," he said, interrupting Dina, who was filling a basket with panda-ear headbands. She looked extra cute in a shiny black dress, cinched at the waist with a white belt. "Elyse is here with food." She turned and looked at me. The panda ears she was wearing on her head only added to her look of surprised innocence.

"Elyse," she said. "Hi. Um. Damien's here!" Like I hadn't noticed.

"I brought pandas," I said flatly, setting the cardboard box down on the kitchen floor. "I don't know where you want them."

"Oh. Awesome," Dina said. "Damien, Elyse brought stuffed pandas." I was sure he was aware. After all, he was standing right behind me. "Would you mind putting them out?"

"Putting them out where?"

"Just out. Places. Put them places. All around." She picked up the box, shoving it into his arms. "Thanks. You're the best." As soon as he was gone she turned to me. "Okay. I didn't know he was coming," she said. "He just . . . showed up."

"And you let him in?" I said incredulously. "You know, some people would call just showing up and inviting yourself in trespassing. If you want me to tell him to leave, I will. Or I can ask Ron Stevenson and the other guys from the football team to show him the door. If he still won't go, we'll call the police."

"No. Elyse." She bit at her lip. "I was actually kind of . . . happy to see him."

"You were *what*? Are you nuts? Do I need to remind you how he treated you?"

"I know." Dina opened a Tupperware and started to arrange the pinwheel cookies on a white plate. "But the thing is, I think he's changed."

I sighed. Didn't Dina ever learn? Guys like that *never* changed. "And what would make you think that?"

"You remember that day when he didn't text me back for sixteen hours?" How could I forget? "Well, when he finally did write back, and I didn't answer for two days, he realized something."

"That he's a jerk?" I supplied.

"That he missed me," she said, still focusing on the cookies instead of looking me in the eye. "He apologized, and we've been texting ever since."

"You've been *what*?" I said again. All those text messages that were supposedly from Dina's newly tech-savvy mother were suddenly making sense. "Why didn't you tell me?"

"Because you hate him," she answered, fussing with the cookies. "And because you really wanted to set me up with Patrick. I didn't want to disappoint you."

"You mean you don't like Patrick?" My worries about Damien suddenly took a backseat.

"He's great, Elyse. Honestly. Such a nice guy. But I just don't feel that spark with him, you know?"

"I thought you said you could see yourself with him five years from now. You said you had real feelings for him."

"I was *trying* to have real feelings for him. I think I just said that stuff to convince myself, because I wanted to feel that way. To make you happy." I almost laughed out loud. If she only knew how miserable the thought of her and Patrick together had been making me. "Damien really *is* sorry for how he treated me," she said, turning away from the cookies to look at me. "You know, I think he just got to college and got overwhelmed by it. All the freedom."

"And all the girls," I added sharply.

"Please don't be mad at him, Elyse," Dina pleaded. She looked like she was about to cry, but I couldn't help it. I wanted to shake her. I wanted to make her see: She was just setting herself up to get hurt. If this was the choice she was making, she wasn't going to get a happy ending. Also, I was mad that she'd lied to me. I thought we were good friends—*best* friends. I thought she trusted me enough to always tell me the truth. "I really appreciate everything you did to try to set me up with Patrick," Dina said. "I hope he finds the right girl for him, but Damien's the guy for me. I can't change that, Elyse, and I don't want to fight against it anymore. So please. Please don't be mad."

I gulped. Then again, I hadn't exactly been honest with Dina, had I? Plus, what did I know about guys? Here I'd thought Patrick was just like the rest of them, and he'd gone and proven me wrong. What's to say I wasn't wrong about Damien, too? For Dina's sake, I hoped I was.

I stepped toward her and sighed. "How could I be mad at you?" I put a hand on her shoulder. "You're dressed like a panda bear." I tweaked her ears. "You'd have to be some kind of monster to be mad at a panda bear. Also, you're my best friend. Whatever you want—even if it's

Damien—that's what I want for you." Her eyes teared up and she launched herself at me, squeezing me tightly.

I hugged her back.

"But, Dina," I said, pulling away suddenly, realizing things weren't all good yet, "is Patrick here?"

"He's upstairs with Jax, rehearsing."

"Oh no." I bit at my thumbnail. "He likes you, Dina. I mean *really* likes you. A lot. You know that song he's going to sing tonight? In front of everyone? It's all about you." She clapped a hand over her mouth.

"Oh my God," she said. "He can't do that. He'll be so embarrassed."

"You're right," I said. "He can't do that. We've got to stop him."

A moment later, the music faded out. A familiar voice started to echo over a microphone. "Check. Check one, two. Can everyone hear me?"

"Oh no," Dina and I said, both at the same time. We raced toward the living room. The hallway was crowded, though, and by the time we got there, we were too late. Patrick obviously wasn't one of those musicians who took two hours to do a sound check. He'd already started.

"Thank you all for coming tonight to celebrate Valentine's Day and save the pandas," he said. "We're the Duotangs." There was a smattering of applause. "I'm going to start by singing you a song I really love." He strummed a chord on his guitar. Even through my panic, I noticed how handsome he looked in an untucked white button-down shirt and black pants. "This is my man Jax on bass," he said. Everyone clapped again. "And this is Van Morrison's 'Brown Eyed Girl.'"

Dina and I both breathed a sigh of relief as Patrick started to strum the familiar tune. Obviously, he'd chickened out. Maybe he'd seen Dina and Damien together and decided against singing the song he wrote. Whatever the reason was, it didn't matter. Everybody who'd ever heard it loved "Brown Eyed Girl." And even if he was singing about Dina, with her big brown eyes, nobody would ever guess.

Plus, another reason to feel relieved: Patrick was good. Really good. He had nothing to be embarrassed about. His voice was deep and steady. And when they came to the "sha-la-la-la-la" parts, he and Jax both closed their eyes and gave it everything they had. His curly hair bounced as he dipped his head to pick out the chords on his guitar. The panda ears he was wearing (Dina had obviously gotten to him earlier) looked ridiculous, but somehow that made me adore him even more. I knew he was singing to Dina, but I wished they were my brown eyes he was serenading.

One by one, couples got up to dance, and everyone joined in singing the chorus. Even Dina and I sang as we linked arms and swayed. Then when the song ended everyone went berserk, screaming and clapping.

"Thank you. Thank you," Patrick and Jax said, waving the applause away. I suddenly wasn't so worried about Patrick anymore. Even if he was about to get his heart broken by Dina, he'd been right. After hearing him sing, every girl at the party was going to be throwing herself at his feet. He'd need all fifteen of those valentines he'd bought. And—even if I hadn't already lost it by acting like such a jerk the other night—there'd be no way I'd be holding on to my spot at number twelve.

"I'm glad you liked the warm-up," Patrick said when the applause had quieted down a bit. "Now I want to take things down a notch and do a little acoustic number." He strummed his guitar again. "I wrote this one myself."

"No. No, no!" I yelled, jumping to my feet.

"Elyse. Hey!" he said, smiling and squinting into the stage lights he and Jax had set up.

Everyone was looking at me now. "Hey," I said lamely, waving to the room in general. "Um, hi." I wanted to tell him he didn't have to go ahead with our "extreme songwriting" deal; that he was only going to humiliate himself in front of this entire room full of people, but now, with everyone staring at us, I realized it would be even more humiliating to stop him. It was going to be like watching a train wreck happen, but there was nothing else I could do.

"Did you say something?" he asked.

"Oh. No," I answered, fumbling for words. "I mean. Yeah. I said snow. Snow. Snow, snow." I pointed out the front window where, mercifully, big white flakes had started to fall. "It's romantic, right? All this snow? Happy Valentine's Day, everyone." I sat back down, feeling like an idiot.

Patrick strummed his guitar again. "Yeah," he said. "Gotta love that snow. Happens every winter."

Everyone kind of laughed, which was fine. I deserved it. I sank farther into my chair. Dina grabbed my hand for support.

"Anyway, a friend of mine once told me," Patrick went on, "that if you like someone, you should tell them in your own words." He looked directly at me, which only made me feel like more of a loser. "So I wrote this song. It's for someone who, in just a short time, has become more special to me than I ever could have thought." He strummed another chord. "Jax here is going to be accompanying me on kazoo and car keys." Everyone laughed again as Jax held up a set of keys and started to shake them rhythmically. "I call this 'Number-One Valentine.'" There was a hush in the room as they started to play.

A dozen roses, a dozen tries, a dozen disappointing valentines
You can see she's feeling sad but you know she'd never say.
She's waiting for the bus, doesn't know my name
Wish her brown eyes would look my way.

Yeah, the girl with the glasses is my number-one valentine.

Jax started in on a kazoo solo. Everyone was swaying. A few people were even waving their lit cell phone screens in the darkened room, like you'd do at a concert.

But I was frozen to the spot, staring directly at Patrick, who was staring directly at me.

A heart-shaped cookie, a heart-shaped sign, the heart she holds is the one that's mine
Though she seems so close she's also far away.
See, she doesn't believe I'm not the same
Wouldn't break her heart, wouldn't go astray.

Yeah, the girl with the glasses is my number-one valentine.

Patrick still hadn't taken his eyes off me, and by now, people had noticed. Everyone who wasn't fixated on Patrick had turned to look at me. A few of the girls were even making schmoopy eyes and nudging their boyfriends. Some stupid person in the back kept saying, "Awwww. That's so sweet." I glanced over my shoulder, trying to silence them with my eyes.

One last try, one last song, one last chance to prove her wrong
Wish I knew the perfect thing to say.
If she turns me down it'll be a shame
But I've gotta take a chance, gotta do it today.

'Cause the girl with the glasses is my number-one valentine.
She's got the keys to my heart, she's my number-one valentine.

He strummed three chords, looking deep into my eyes from across the room—as if nobody else were there.

She don't come by the dozen, she's my number-one valentine.

When he'd played the last chord, the room fell silent. *Everyone,* and I mean everyone, was watching him, watching me. Or watching me watching him, waiting to see what we'd do next. Patrick lifted his guitar strap over his head and gently handed the instrument to Jax. He took a single step toward me.

I stood up. "Excuse me," I said, pushing past a girl, nearly spilling the glass of pop she was holding. "Excuse me," I said again. I could feel that tears were streaming down my cheeks, but I didn't have time to wipe them off. "Get out of the way!" I shouted at a guy who didn't move fast enough. I could feel Patrick's eyes—everyone's eyes—still on me and I couldn't breathe. I just couldn't breathe. My only thought was that I had to get to the door.

Chapter 18

By the time he reached me I was already fumbling with my keys. "Elyse!" Patrick said. "Wait."

"No," I answered, finally getting the car door open.

"Please. Just listen to me for a minute."

I turned on him. My voice came out shaky and furious. "You're supposed to like Dina," I said, tears still running down my face.

"I am?" he said.

"Yes," I accused. "You bought her favorite valentine with the stupid hat-wearing puppies on it. You helped her with the music for the party as an excuse to get her number. You told me she was pretty. You even asked if she was single." I pointed toward the living room where he'd just surprised me in front of everyone at the panda party. "So what the hell was that?"

"That was a song I wrote. For you." Like it wasn't obvious. Like every single person at the party didn't know exactly how he felt now. "I thought it would be romantic."

Romantic? Try overwhelming? Try mind-boggling? Try

the rug's just been pulled out from underneath me and I don't know whether to laugh or cry kind of shocking? I knew what he'd done was sweet, not to mention brave. I should have been happy, I guessed, and I was, but I was also embarrassed, and confused. I hadn't had time to sort it all out in my mind yet.

"Jax said he thought any girl would like it," Patrick tried. Then he sighed, letting his shoulders drop. He rubbed his hand across his forehead as if trying to figure me out was giving him a major headache. "But then again, Jax is nineteen, and he's never had a girlfriend, so . . . God, I'm sorry, Elyse. I suck at this stuff. I know I told you that one time in the car I'd had tons of girlfriends back in Toronto, but that wasn't exactly true. More like two. Or, okay, two and a half if you count this girl I shared an ice cream with at summer camp when I was twelve. Plus, I'm totally dense. You already told me that day in the car: You don't feel the same way I do. I just thought maybe it wouldn't hurt to give it one last shot. I've been trying to just be your friend, but I haven't been able to get you off my mind."

He reached into his back pocket. "And for whatever it's worth, I got you this." He passed me an envelope. I took it and tore it open. Inside was my favorite valentine from Goodman's Gifts & Stationery—the blank card with the red heart on a silver background. I flipped it open. Inside were the lyrics of the song he'd just sung for me. "I wrote it myself, and it actually rhymes," he added miserably. "I thought you'd like that." I looked up at him. The streetlight caught the snowflakes in his hair, making it sparkle. He was so gorgeous, and so sweet, and so clueless all at the same time. "Oh yeah," he said, misunderstanding my gaze. He reached up and took off his panda ears headband. "And here I am, confessing my love while wearing panda ears. Just add that to my list of smooth moves."

"What are you talking about?"

"What do you mean, what am I talking about? Every time I try to do something nice for you, I screw it up." He started to list things off on his fingers. "I freak you out with a parallel parking lesson, tell you you killed my grandfather's favorite blossoming Japanese cherry bush, bake you inedible cookies, give you dead flowers, tease you about accidentally shutting off your furnace, scare you half to death by banging garbage can lids together, make you break your phone. . . ." He trailed off. "And, oh yeah, now it turns out I led you to believe I had the hots for your friend, plus I embarrassed you in front of a room full of people. I'm sure you're just dying to go out with me. Who wouldn't be? Patrick Connor over here," he shouted, loud enough for the whole street to hear. "Total catch!" He put his panda ears back on. "Tonight only, comes with dorky panda ears."

"Shut up," I said softly.

Did he honestly think that I cared about any of that? Didn't he realize I'd been so much worse, pushing him away every time he tried to help me; constantly assuming that, just because he was a guy, he was a pig like Matt Love when, really, he was the complete opposite? Didn't he know how much I wished I could have taken what he was offering—the thoughtful gestures and even the cheesy romantic stuff—without feeling like I was just handing my heart over to be crushed?

"So then after you got mad at me, I just tried to do stuff for you in secret, because at least then you wouldn't be disappointed if I messed it up. But, knowing me, I probably screwed it up anyway. Like the driveway—you probably didn't want it shoveled. And the Cupid doll. I probably gave it to the wrong sick baby. And then, after the whole stupid thing with the Lyme disease, I went and lied about having scurvy, which is a real disease brought on by a vitamin deficiency, you know. It's not something to joke about."

"Shut up," I said again.

"Right. Shutting up." He turned, but I put a hand on his shoulder, stopping him in his tracks. Before he could have known what was happening, and before I even had a chance to think about it, I was in front of him. And I was kissing him. At first he must have been shocked. His arms hung limply at his sides, but a second later, I felt one of his hands on my back, then moving up my shoulders. His fingers brushed the back of my head lightly. I thought he was going to run his fingers through my hair—all passionate and romantic—but a second later, I felt what he was really doing: sliding his panda ears onto my head. I pulled away and looked up, laughing. "Thanks," I said, straightening them.

"You're welcome," Patrick said, obviously trying to assess the situation. We stood there, looking into each other's eyes. "Can I take what just happened to mean you don't hate me?"

"I don't hate you," I answered.

"Okay." He hesitated. "Can I take it to mean that you like me?"

"I like you," I told him.

"You do? I like you, too," he answered.

"Yeah. I kind of figured," I said. "From the song . . ."

"And Dina? She's nice. And yeah, even pretty, but I don't feel that way about her. I was helping her out with the music as a way to be closer to *you*. The reason I asked if she was single . . . that was for Jax."

He looked toward the front window of Dina's house. Inside, I could see Patrick's coworker, Jax, coiling up different cables. "He's really into saving the whales," Patrick explained. I remembered the tattoo of the killer whale I'd seen on his arm the day I'd gone looking for Patrick at the Keyhole. "I thought maybe they'd get along. I don't know. Combine forces and save some new animal. Sea horses, or something. You never see anyone saving them. But it looks like she's interested in that older guy who showed up. So . . ."

"Too bad for the sea horses," I supplied. Jax seemed like a really nice guy. I had no doubt, at least, he would have treated Dina better than Damien did. But what could you do?

"Yeah. Rotten luck for the sea horses." Patrick paused. "So. You like me?" he asked again, like he still didn't believe what I was saying.

"Yes," I answered, laughing. "I like you. Come here." I grabbed his hand and led him around to the back of the car. "I made you a present." I opened the trunk and lifted the lid off a cardboard box.

"You did this?" he asked, leaning down to look at the huge layer cake I'd made. The top was decorated with tiny icing roadways. Buildings and houses made of shortbread cookies lined the streets, and matchbox cars zoomed along the roads.

"This one here is an Audi A4," I said, pointing to a car. "It'd run you about forty thousand dollars. And here's the BMW 7-Series. Eighty thousand minimum." He blushed. "And here I am"—I pointed to a small red car between them—"extreme parallel parking between them, and passing my road test with a near-perfect score."

"Did you really?" he asked, beaming.

"I really did." He hugged me. "And here," I said, turning back to the cake and pointing out the lettering at the bottom, "is where it says 'Thank you, Patrick' because I realized I never said that to you in person. Not sincerely, anyway. And I should have. Even if I'd failed my road test, I still owe you huge just for believing in me and refusing to give up, even when I wasn't exactly always nice to you. I'm not so great at accepting help from people," I admitted. "Or dealing with big, romantic gestures. I guess I'm kind of working on that."

He smiled and stuck his finger in the icing, licking it clean. "Can I eat it?" he asked after the fact.

"Well, yeah. Now that you licked it."

"Awesome. Can we bring it inside first? My feet are about to fall off." I looked down and noticed for the first time that he'd been in such a rush to run after me that he hadn't even put his boots on.

I reached into the trunk for the cake. "Here," Patrick said, getting in front of me. "I'll get it."

"I can—" I started, then stopped myself. I took a step back. "Thanks," I said, letting him lift it out. I slammed the trunk closed, leaned over the cake box he was holding, and kissed him once more, softly on the lips. It was a long, slow, lingering kiss, but the second I pulled my lips away, he ran up the walkway, stopping halfway and hopping around frantically on the balls of his feet while he waited for me to catch up. He had an enormous grin on his face, and it was hard to tell if he was bouncing around like that because his feet were cold, or because he was happy . . . but if how I was feeling myself was any indication, I was willing to bet it had more to do with option two.

Epilogue

One and a half years later . . .

"Patrick!" I yelled, leaning out my bedroom window. "Jax! Would you shut that thing off and go get ready?"

My gorgeous, curly-haired boyfriend looked up at me from the backyard, smiling. "But we've almost got it working perfectly. Look." He turned to his friend who, by now, was as much my friend. "Okay, Jax. Really get into character. *Be* the raccoon."

Jax made rings with his fingers and held them up over his eyes, crouching down low and sneaking across the yard. He approached the garbage bins, sniffing at the air as if smelling delicious, rotting things. But when he went to lift the lid of the organic waste bin, a 200-watt floodlight instantly flicked on, an automated motion-detector sprinkler system kicked in, and incredibly loud soft-rock music filled the air (Céline Dion's "My Heart Will Go On"). Patrick didn't have any real proof, but he was convinced this particular song would send the two raccoons—who had built a nest in the roof of our shed and given birth to six young—packing. They'd taught themselves to undo the raccoon-proof garbage straps the spring after Patrick had installed them for me and, since then, my mom, Patrick, and I had been locked in an epic battle with them.

Jax fake-screeched and ran away, his clothes dripping sprinkler water.

I couldn't help the laugh that escaped my lips, but I stifled it quickly. "Shut it off!" I yelled over the music. "You guys, you're getting the grass wet! The ceremony's only an hour away!" A small circle of chairs was already set up at the far end of the yard near the Japanese cherry tree, which was in full bloom.

"Oh. Right," Patrick said. "Sorry!" He turned off the sprinkler. "So?" He stood back. "What do you think?"

"It's impressive," I answered. "It's great, really. I love it." There was a knock at my door. "Now go." I shooed Patrick and Jax away. "Get dressed."

"Going," Patrick answered. "See you soon, raccoon." He blew me a kiss, which I pretended to ignore.

"I'm decent. Come in," I yelled in the direction of my door, figuring it was my mother, or maybe Dina arriving early to show me her dress. Since she and Damien had finally broken up the month before (something that had been a long time coming, if you asked me), she'd been planning her outfit for this day, hoping to look so hot Jax would be forced to see her as more than just a friend. I had a feeling she wouldn't have a hard time. He'd had a crush on her for ages. But even though she'd long since stopped being mad at me for trying to set her up with

Patrick when I liked him myself, she refused to let me play any part in setting her up with his best friend.

"No offense," she'd said, "but your matchmaking skills are worse than your driving skills used to be." She was right, and I didn't take it personally.

But it wasn't Dina at the door. "What's that? Didn't quite hear you," a familiar voice answered. I slid the window shut and crossed the room.

"Mr. Connor! I mean, Frank." I was more than a little surprised to see Patrick's grandfather standing in the hallway outside my bedroom, already dressed in his suit. Since Patrick and I had started dating, our families had become close, and he stopped by often to have tea with me or my mom. But his arthritis was getting worse. He didn't usually climb our steep stairs if he could avoid it.

"Oh, well," he said, taking me in. "Don't you look lovely, Elyse." I stepped back to let him in, enjoying the way my long, silk dress rippled around my ankles. "I wanted to bring this by." He pressed something into my hand. I looked down at the tiny heart-shaped opal pendant. "Something old. Something blue. Something borrowed. It's been a long time since there's been a wedding in this house," he said.

"Thank you." I hugged him tightly.

After I helped Mr. Connor down the stairs, I came back and sat on my bed, holding the pendant in my hand and marveling at how much had changed since Valentine's Day a year and a half ago.

For one thing, Dina and I had both been fired. It happened the day after Dina's party, when Mr. Goodman discovered the empty chocolate box in the storage room and talked to a few customers. He was *really* disappointed in us, even after we explained that we'd stolen the chocolates for the greater good of the forest-dwelling bears of China. And while he didn't take our pay bonuses away (between that and the party, Dina raised enough money to adopt Oreo *and* his sister Domino), he did say that he couldn't condone our behavior, and that keeping us on would send the wrong message to the rest of the staff.

It was upsetting at first, but in the long run it worked out. Dina got a part-time job cleaning cages and coordinating adoptions at Piggies in Crisis, a local guinea pig rescue organization. And, as for me, I found a woman in our area who ran a cake-baking business and needed help in the afternoons icing cakes and doing deliveries. I loved the work—not to mention the free cake I got to bring home sometimes—and the customers were great, too. Mrs. Conchetti even ordered a heart-shaped cake from us last February, to celebrate her grandson's first birthday.

And then there was my boyfriend . . . sweet, loyal, loving Patrick, who—when he wasn't busy building me state-of-the-art raccoon deterrent systems—could usually be found helping my mom change the oil in our car, or stopping by Piggies in Crisis with a fresh load of free woodchips for Dina. Even though he'd graduated from high school and was busier than ever doing an apprenticeship as a cabinetmaker, he never passed up an opportunity to help anyone with anything. He also never stopped trying to get the whole romance thing right: a candlelit dinner with home-cooked chicken à la king for my birthday (which I pretended not to notice was almost too dry to eat), surprise cards and flowers for no reason at all, picnics in the park. Even though I kept telling him I didn't need that stuff, the truth was, it made him so happy to do it for me that I'd almost grown to like it.

Even his over-the-top helpfulness seemed charming to me most of the time these days, but there was still the odd time when he made me sigh in exasperation. Like the day last month when he oh-so-helpfully stopped by the house on his lunch break and checked our mail, then drove halfway across the city to find me at school, interrupting a last-minute cramming session before my calculus exam.

"Elyse!" he'd said, kissing me on the cheek before sliding onto the bench of the cafeteria table with so much enthusiasm he nearly knocked me to the floor. "It's here. Open it. Open it right now." I'd held up one finger, then finished the equation I'd been working on before setting my calculus book down carefully. "Please!" he'd said, bouncing around like a kid waiting to open a birthday present. "You're killing me here. Open it."

I'd looked over at him with trepidation. After all, the contents of that envelope could easily change everything—and not necessarily for the better. "*You* open it," I'd said, then winced as he tore the paper. The crinkling noise of the letter unfolding had somehow seemed magnified, even in the noisy cafeteria.

"Hmmm." He scrunched up his face as he read. "Well . . ."

"Give me that!" I'd grabbed it from him.

"You did it!" A grin spread across his face. "A full scholarship." Then he'd pulled me to my feet and hugged me before lifting me up and twirling me around. "My girlfriend is the smartest person in the entire world!" he'd yelled to the whole cafeteria.

Since then, Patrick had helped me to prepare in a dozen different ways: visiting the campus with me, poring over course calendars, making phone calls to look for a student apartment, booking a moving van. But nothing he did could really prepare either one of us for the reality we'd be facing in just a few short months. I'd be heading off to college in upstate New York. He'd be staying in Middleford, continuing his apprenticeship and looking after his grandfather. We'd see each other in the summers, and over the holidays, of course. But I couldn't imagine how that would be enough. We'd barely spent a day apart in the last year and a half. Then again, I decided, it would just have to be enough—because I couldn't stand the thought of losing him. I loved Patrick more than I'd ever thought possible.

"Elyse?" Another knock at the door interrupted my thoughts. "Can I come in?"

My mother didn't wait for an answer. She stepped into the room. Her hair was arranged in careful ringlets and she looked more beautiful than I'd ever seen her. Like all the heroines in the sappy romantic comedies she watched, she looked radiant and hopeful—ready to enjoy her happily ever after.

"Oh, Mom." I stood up.

She twirled in her antique lace dress, seeming kind of embarrassed. "Thanks, sweetie."

"I've got something for you from Mr. Connor," I said, opening my palm to show her the necklace. "Something old, blue, and borrowed. Here, turn around." I lifted her curls and fastened the clasp of the opal pendant around her neck, then stepped back to take in the full picture. She looked stunning in the cream-colored dress, and the iridescent aqua color of the pendant brought out the blue flecks in her eyes, just like it had the times I'd worn it. "Are you nervous?" I asked.

"Not as nervous as Valter is," she said, laughing.

As it turned out, what happened in Mexico *didn't* stay in Mexico. Not by a long shot. At first, I'd resented Valter—the way he'd tried to befriend me with offers of ice cream (like I was a five-year-old), the nights he and my mother stayed out late dancing like they were the ones who were teenagers, and, worse, the times he spent the night and I'd wake to find him in our kitchen, pouring himself a bowl of cereal like he owned the place. But, over time, I'd come not to mind him as much. If Valter Bigaskis made my mother happy—and he did—then who was I to stand in the way?

I looked at the clock. "Okay. You ready?"

"As ready as I'll ever be," my mom answered. We hugged each other once, then started down the stairs.

"Here they come," I heard Patrick say as our feet hit the creaky third stair from the top.

"What's that?" Patrick's grandfather asked loudly. "You want some gum?" But then he saw us and his eyes got a faraway look. "Well, now I can say I've seen the two most beautiful brides in the world come down that staircase," he told my mother. She blushed.

When my mom had asked Patrick's grandfather to walk her down the aisle, he'd been overjoyed, but when she'd told him she'd be saying her vows with Valter under the same flowering Japanese cherry tree as he and Jeannie had, he'd been so touched that he'd nearly cried.

"Shall we, Michelle?" My mother reached for Frank's arm and he led her into the kitchen.

Patrick came forward next, took me by the hand, and twirled me around. "You look beautiful," he said.

I smiled at him in his suit. "You don't look so bad yourself," I answered, kissing him softly on the lips.

"You know, Elyse . . ." He hesitated, pulling back and giving me a serious look. "It's *still* not too late for you to reconsider."

I headed over to the hallway mirror to straighten the chain on my necklace—a small pearl pendant Patrick had given me on our first anniversary/Valentine's Day. He came up behind me, lacing his arms around my waist and looking over my shoulder. "Elyse Big-ass-kiss," I said, trying to keep a straight face. I cleared my throat. "I'm a member of the Big-ass-kiss family." I winced. "Nice to meet you." I extended my hand toward the mirror. "I'm a Big-ass-kiss." Patrick snorted, covering his mouth. Thankfully, my mother was out of earshot in the kitchen, fussing with her bouquet.

"Hmmm." Patrick made a pained face.

"Yeah," I agreed. "Not so much."

"Well then, Elyse *Ulrich,*" he said, holding out his arm the same way his grandfather had done for my mother. "Shall we?"

"Yes, Patrick Connor, I think we shall," I answered. Then we linked arms and walked out into the sunshine toward the waiting guests.